Twist of Fate

By

Shawna C. Jones

ISBN: 978-0-9913984-2-3.

Dedicated to starseeds everywhere

Preface

This novel is based on a true story of my life, with my spiritual journey bumping into my physical journey. The dreams I had back then came true in various ways. They continue to this day. For those who can relate to this, you know what I'm talking about. Dreams of death, or knowing when someone is going to die, is both a blessing and a curse.

This is a story I never wanted to write; however, I attended a writer's seminar which changed my mind. During the seminar, we meditated and were told that whichever book showed up, was the one our soul wanted to write. I had already written another book and was sure it would be the one to show up. Instead, I was given the story you are about to read. In fact John, an important character, handed it to me in a gold box!

To protect the privacy of those involved, I have changed all of the characters' names, including my own; I also changed some of their physical characteristics and nationalities, as well as a couple of the story's locations. Most of what I've written is true including a lot of the conversations. I did not want to write this story as a memoir because it would have had too many characters, been too long, and exposed too many details of the characters that are better left unsaid.

So put on your backpack and get ready, because we're going places. I hope you enjoy the ride!

Shawna C. Jones

Prologue

I travel to cope with my inner demon. An inner demon that was revealed to me when I was five years old.

As I was sitting on a swing in my parents' backyard, a strange thought occurred to me out of nowhere.

"*My parents are not my parents. There has been a huge mistake and I am in the wrong place, the wrong everything.*" I was so upset that I obsessed over this thought. I wondered if I had been adopted at first, but realized it was not true. I looked too much like them.

As I thought about it for some time, I realized another message: *this is not my real home; I don't belong here.* This message became etched into my consciousness, or perhaps it had always been there, and I was only now aware of it. Either way, it would direct my life, for better or for worse. One thing became certain—I would seek to find my true home, my real home, even if I had to travel thousands of miles or die trying.

And it would have to be my secret. One I couldn't tell anyone, at least not yet.

So at twenty-one years of age, I would start my journey to faraway places...

Chapter 1

I was in my bedroom, packing clothes into a medium-sized backpack for my first trip to Europe. I was excited and slightly anxious at the same time, but it also felt great to be going somewhere different. The sun was shining on this September day, and the heat and humidity was still alive and well, in the hell that I call Miami. My older sister Gina, who looks a lot like me, flopped down on my bed and critically looked at what I was doing.

"You have too many clothes in there," she said, as I tried to stuff more into my already overstuffed backpack. "Why are you traveling for so long? Most people travel for a month at most, and you're going for a year. I hope you know what you're doing."

She made a face at me and I could sense her jealousy. I was going to do something that she'd never had the nerve to do. Her negativity was a cover for her own insecurity and fear.

"I know what I'm doing. Besides, I didn't work two full-time jobs for nothing. I did that so I could take the time off. I look at it as running towards my future, unlike most of the stick-in-the-muds around here." I continued to struggle with the backpack, and the clothes flew out. I sighed and unloaded the rest of them back on the bed.

"Most people prefer the word *settle*. It's safe for

people to stay in one place and not think about other possibilities. I'm quite content to stay here in Miami, but I know you hate it here. I just don't understand why."

"I don't hate it. It just doesn't feel like home to me. Never has. I've always wanted a different type of life than what I see around here. It's so boring here: get married, work, have children, give up your life. The young people hang out at the beach, party, and do drugs. That's just not for me. And look at Mom. Don't you think she gave up a lot to stay home? Her longings and dreams got put on hold a long time ago, and she never found the passion again. I don't want to live like that."

"Staying in one place doesn't have to be boring," Gina argued. "Your problem is that you're a free spirit and independent, plus you don't like having any strings attached to you. You think every place or thing is a prison. School was a prison, living here is a prison, marriage is a prison. I rest my case."

"You sound like a lawyer. Just like Dad. And yes, school was a twelve-year sentence that I endured to get my education. Higher education will buy my freedom. I already have two trades as a computer programmer and a secretary, but neither one seem to be my calling. One gives me more money, and the other gives me a chance to interact with the public--unlike you, who will stay in one job forever."

"And what about California and Sam?" Gina said, her

blue eyes glaring at me. "Was *he* a prison as well?" She tossed her long blonde hair behind her, a sure sign that she was itching for a fight. I decided not to indulge her.

"Sam picked drugs over me, and that ended that relationship. But California is a great place. I came home to save money so I could travel. Another short-term prison sentence, and now I'm paroled." I smiled as I said this. I would soon have an adventure and freedom.

I didn't tell her that I'd felt like I just didn't belong with him anymore. That it was the first time I had been acutely aware of my inner demon.

"Maybe you should be a flight attendant?" Our mother, Elizabeth, stood in the doorway, eyeing both of us. Her short curly brown hair adorned her sweet oval face. For a "fake mother" she had turned out to be pretty good, even if she'd never understood me. Her jeans and tee shirt were slightly dirty from working out in the garden.

"I thought of that. But then I'd be stuck in a home base I might not like, and traveling to places for only short jaunts. It just isn't long enough."

I now had the clothes in sections and only picked the ones I could layer. I would be doing the laundry, so it was imperative that I take as few things as possible.

"I think you're running away from something. I just don't know what it is." My sister got up off the bed and walked out the door before I could answer.

"Is that true, Shawna?" asked Mom.

"No, it's not. I'm actually a seeker. An adventurer, if you will. I just want excitement in my life. You know I get restless. Change is good. I don't understand why people resist it."

I now had the backpack full of clothes and personal items, with room to spare. Shawna: 1. Backpack: 1.

"We should head down soon. Your dad and Aunt Emma will be here shortly."

I watched her slim figure walk away while she shook her head. I knew she worried about me, but I knew deep down I would be fine. I had beliefs that I was putting to the test: Europe would be a great place and I would be safe, life is an adventure so live it, and anything I ask the Universe for, I would receive.

I looked in the mirror at my blonde hair and blue eyes. I'd lost weight from working long hours and not eating as much. I could stand to gain a few pounds but was happy how I looked. My face was oval-shaped, with high cheekbones and clear skin. Everyone always asked what I used to get such great skin, and I shared my beauty secrets with them: no smoking, no drugs, healthy diet, exercise, and good genes. Plus stay out of the sun or use sunscreen. Difficult to do in Miami, but I was glad our pool had plenty of shade around it.

My sister and I were fortunate. I never had problems getting male attention, whether I wanted it or not. Neither did she, yet deep down I knew she was envious of me. I could leave anyone or anything without thinking about it. My secret allowed me to do that. She would stay in relationships longer than she wanted. In fact, she had a hard time with breakups. I was glad that Sam and I had broken off our engagement; it freed me up for my new obsession: travel. I wanted to find my real home and add some excitement to my life.

I combed my hair and headed downstairs.

Aunt Emma and Dad were already in the living room, talking with Gina and Mom. Mom and Aunt Emma resembled each other, and were very close—friends as well as family. But Aunt Emma and I also shared a secret. We both were intuitive. My mother, not as much, and my sister, not at all. I had dreams that came true. Most of them dealing with death. It still shocked me when the death happened, though. I'd been given a gift and had no way of coping with it. The dreams haunted me and I always felt guilty when the death happened. But I knew I couldn't stop the event from happening, Aunt Emma and other mediums had assured me of that. I could simply observe and know the future. Other events sometimes showed up as well, but one particular dream, a skydiving dream, always left me cold. I hadn't been able to talk about it, but then a few months ago Aunt Emma suspected something was wrong. When she confronted me, I told her about it. My secret was safe with her.

"You look great. Like a woman ready for an

adventure. Are you scared to be traveling on your own?" she asked. She sat on the sofa with my sister and mother. My father, William, was relaxed in his recliner. He was a tall, good-looking man in his early forties. He and my mother had met in Kansas, but chose to live in Florida after they were married in Kansas. Now *there's* a place I never wanted to live. Florida was better, but not by much. The heat and humidity killed me, but the cold would have been worse. While I merely survived the heat, my sister and parents thrived in it. I felt out of place and different from them, but at least I wasn't stuck here.

"I'm a little scared, but more excited. I have my guidebooks and maps to get me in the right direction, hopefully. I'm going to places I've always wanted to go to," I said enthusiastically. "London's been calling me for years." I had been having dreams of England and other parts of Europe for quite some time. I wanted to follow my dreams, and hoped for thrills and action to offset the mundane life in Miami.

"Good." My aunt winked at me. I knew she thought my intuition would serve me well. It had been preordained by other seers. This explorer had a mission in life.

"Do you have your work visa?" asked Dad, sipping a beer.

"Yes. My UK visa is in good order. London is a good transition to the rest of Europe. At least they speak English. Then I'm off to Holland to buy a car and drive down to Spain. From there I go to the Canary Islands, and then who knows?"

"What about your will? Not something we like to talk about, but you never know. Young people think they'll live forever, but you never know what could happen."

 I shuddered at the thought. Not for me, but because his words reminded me of my dream.

"Yes, as is my life insurance. All of you are beneficiaries."

"Good. Then I hope you die," said Gina laughing. Everyone looked at her, shocked, but I only laughed.

"Spoken like a true sister. The good news is I'm not afraid to die. Not now, not ever. And I don't have a lot. At least not yet."

"Well, let's not talk about death and destruction. Goodness, you've haven't left home yet and already we're planning your funeral," said Aunt Emma. "Let's hope you live to a ripe old age."

"I'll drink to that." My dad held up glass of beer. Everyone else had wine or tea. We raised our containers.

"May the Irish elves smile down on you and guide you on your way," said Mom, with a wistful look in her eyes.

"Yes. I could use some elves and angels on this trip. And I know they are there."

I've learned lessons in my life, and the one that helped me on my first day of travel was this: Trust your intuition. Always. It would come in handy throughout my

Twist of Fate

journey.

Chapter 2

After an uneventful flight, the 747 landed at Heathrow Airport. As I entered the enormous terminal, I thought that it might as well have been the U.N., for I saw people of every nationality and heard every imaginable language. I watched passengers as I glided through immigration and customs without any problems.

I loved London, even though it seemed like a madhouse. A big, bustling city with so much history and so many activities that I became overwhelmed with choices. I would need years to see and experience this great city. As Samuel Johnson said, "When a man is tired of London, he is tired of life."

There were tubes (subways), and trains to take you anywhere and everywhere you wanted to go. Mobs of people were rushing to catch trains or cabs, running down subway escalators, and walking briskly in the streets. London had a manic beat to it, and I got caught up in it.

As excited as I was about being here, there also seemed to be a familiarity to it. Especially when I stood in the Underground. Hundreds of years of odors swept into my nose; it was a musty smell that was recognizable, if only I could remember. Then the sound and gust of wind blowing hard, then harder, to warn you that the train was getting closer. The wheels on the tracks had a rhythm all their own. It felt good to be home again.

I thought it would be nice to travel with someone for a time, and I got my wish on the subway. An American gal bumped into me when the train lurched forward. She apologized and we exchanged pleasantries.

"I'm Lyn Holmes from California," she said. She had light-brown hair and looked to be the same age as me. She wore jeans and a white tee shirt with a surfboard on it. Her denim jacket covered most of it. She had a cute turned-up nose and green eyes. I liked her instantly.

"I'm Shawna Jones from Florida, for now. But I did live in San Francisco for a year. I really like California." I said, as we stood holding onto the railing of the speeding train.

"Me too." We talked about our life experiences, and she said she would be traveling for at least another year.

"And I thought a year was a long time." I looked at her in wide-eyed amazement. "I'm just starting out. What country did you fly to first?"

"I went to Japan first, and then Asia. I'm just now getting back to Europe. I went home for a few months when my dad got sick, but now I'm resuming my trip."

"What are going to do when you're done?"

"I'm not sure. I haven't found 'the one', if you know what I mean. I have been close though. But either way I'm going to go school when I'm done. Not sure what I'll take.

This is my gift that I'm giving to myself before I have to slog it through school for three or four years. How about you?"

"Your story sounds like my story, but what I really want is an adventure. And I'm looking for a new place to call home, wherever that might be. As soon as my year is up, I'll probably go back to school."

She looked intently at me when I said that, as if reading my mind.

"Home's a tough one. I always ask myself, 'Who am I?' Where am I from?' I get different answers all the time. It seems like we have a lot in common. I bet you'd love Asia. The Buddhist monks have much to teach us."

"One of these days I'll get there. Where are you going now?"

"Sightseeing. You want to go with me? By the way, where are you staying?"

"Traveler's Hostel near Marble Arch. And yes, I'd love to go sightseeing."

"Great. We're at the same hostel, too. So that's terrific." And just like that, I had a new buddy.

London proved to be quite the provider of my needs. At least for the next two weeks, I had someone to travel with.

But when we went to The Tower of London, I got an odd feeling. I actually didn't want to go in. My heart raced and I had fears that turned into an anxiety attack, even though I'd never had one. A feeling of doom and gloom swept over me. A premonition of death overcame me, and I refused to enter. My palms had started sweating and I was in no mood to sightsee.

Lyn grabbed my hand and guided me in, while I protested. Sheer panic had set in. She took me to a small alcove to talk in private.

"Shawna what is going on? Breathe deeply," she said quietly. She stared into my eyes. "Tell me."

"I feel dread. I feel death. I can't go in," I said, staring back at her.

"Who's going to die?" She never took her eyes off mine.

"I think I am. Or did already. I'm not sure anymore."

"Ah. A past life recollection. Nothing to worry about. It happened a long time ago."

"Then why does it feel like yesterday?"

"You're just more in tune to the vibe of this place than most people are. That's all. Maybe the ghost of Queen Anne is waiting for you." She grinned as she said this, to lighten the mood.

"Why did you say Queen Anne?" I took more deep breaths. I felt calmer.

"I don't know why. Strange. I picked up on something around you. But you're ready to move on now, right? After all, we've already paid." I wondered if Lyn was intuitive like me. She certainly acted like it.

16

My breathing had returned to normal. I felt better. Now I wanted to see the Tower more than ever. Curiosity had crept in, making me more determined to keep going.

"I'm sorry about that. I don't know what go into me."

"Don't apologize. You have the ability to feel past events. Many would want that."

"They can have it." I assured her. Then we both laughed, and I started to feel normal again.

Lyn agreed to travel to Amsterdam with me where I would buy a car; then we would head to Belgium, France, and Spain. We had picked out all the cities and sites we wanted to see along the way. We would have to part in Spain, but in the meantime, it was great to have a companion.

Lesson: Feel the fear and do it anyway.

Chapter 3

I never wanted to drive in Paris, yet all roads seemed to lead there. I thought Lyn and I could stop outside the city and take a train instead; but my white Volkswagen appeared to know the route better than I did. Lyn pointed to signs as we passed them, and then looked at the map. She could not drive a stick shift and refused to learn, but she made a great copilot.

"Do I have to drive in Paris?" I moaned to her. "I really don't like traffic and roundabouts."

"You can do it. You've driven in Amsterdam and down through Belgium. And it's not that far now. Just think. Soon we'll be in romantic Paris, and you'll forget all about driving and traffic."

"You know I don't normally drive a stick shift either. So this is really nerve-wracking for me." The freeways were fine, but the idea of driving in Paris terrified me. And yet, I knew I would still do it. Nothing can stop a determined woman from reaching her goal.

"Don't worry. You drive like a pro." I didn't know if she was being sarcastic or not, but I decided to let it slide.

Paris traffic is murder. Hundreds of cars merging into various roundabouts and streets. The roundabouts made me dizzy. No room for error or for changing lanes, it seemed. I constantly looked out for other drivers, pedestrians, bicyclists, and anything out of the ordinary. It was exhausting, and made me regret ever buying a car. I cursed myself for it. Trains would have made traveling easier. But no, the idiot from America had to have her car. Part of the freedom I craved. I would have to get over that.

"There it is. The road we want." Lyn pointed excitedly to a street. "Turn right and we're almost there."

I parked the car and looked around. "I'm never driving in Paris again. Never. Now where is that youth hostel?" I asked impatiently.

"It's supposed to be around here someplace. Let's get out and look." We got out of the car and stretched before continuing along the sidewalk. We immediately met two young men with backpacks looking at a map. They looked lost as they eyed various street signs.

"Do you know where Residence Hostel is?" one of them asked. He had an American accent. He studied his map and pointed to a spot on it. He had long blonde hair, blue eyes, and a beard. I wasn't sure but he looked like a hiker to me.

"We're looking for the same one," I replied. "We're hoping it's down this street." Lyn and I introduced ourselves.

"I'm Mike Talbot and this is John Fontaine." He motioned to his companion.

"So you're French, and you're American? Is that

right?" asked Lyn.

"I'm half French, half English," said John in a heavy British accent. "I grew up in London, but have relatives in France. None in Paris, though." He had longish, dark brown hair and blue eyes. Both were at least six feet, with average builds. John carried a guitar case over his right shoulder.

"We should find this place before it gets dark. I'm certainly not driving in this city at night."

"That's a cute ride. Hope it didn't cost much," said Mike, eyeing the car.

"It was cheap. I paid one-fifty for it in Amsterdam. But now I wish I'd just taken the train."

He nodded, then said, "If I'm not mistaken, the building should be about three or four blocks down the road. We could drive there in the car." I was beginning to not like Mike.

"Maybe we should just walk," I replied.

"We should drive. We'll just have to come back for it later," said Lyn. I gave her a dirty look, which she ignored.

"I'll drive if you don't want to," said John. I smiled at him. He smiled back. Someone who gets it.

"No, it's okay. Let's go. What's one more mile in Paris?" I sighed. The guys hopped into the back seat and tried to put their packs in the trunk. Their packs were larger than ours, but one fit in. John kept his guitar on his lap. Then we were off to the youth hostel.

"This can't be. Are they kidding me?" I asked, looking at the abandoned building with its cracked windows and peeling paint.

"My guidebook doesn't say it's closed," said Mike, "but it is. Should we look around?"

"Might as well," said Lyn. We all got out of the car and cautiously approached the building.

"Is this a safe neighborhood?" I asked. I didn't see anyone about. At least the streetlights worked.

"It's supposed to be." Mike opened the door slowly and peered inside. He motioned for us to enter. It seemed to be in disrepair, but looked like it hadn't been closed for long. A few months at most.

I tried the faucets in the bathroom and kitchen. No water and no electricity. But it did look safe enough to stay in for one night. We searched all the rooms for squatters, and found no one.

"When did you guys start traveling?" I asked. I wanted to share travel experiences.

"About two weeks for me," said Mike.

"Today," said John. "I met Mike on the ferry from Dover to Calais."

"I've been traveling for five weeks. So far all the Europeans have been friendly and nice," I said as I rolled out my sleeping bag. I hope that held true tonight. I decided this place was better than driving around Paris at night looking for another hostel.

Lyn told them her story while she got her sleeping bag in place. The guys did the same, then re-organized their packs. We all slept in the same large room, but Lyn and I kept several feet between ourselves and them.

"It could get pretty cold so I suggest we keep heavier clothes on," said Mike. He told us he had hiked several times in the mountains, and seemed to know a lot about what to do when roughing it.

Our flashlights came on when it got too dark to see. Clearly the great outdoors was now our restroom. We agreed on areas for the guys and for us to use.

I couldn't help but laugh.

"What's so funny?" John asked, grinning at me.

"I worked two full-time jobs for six months so I could camp out. How ironic is that?"

"You must have been determined. I plan to work in places as I travel. I'm on my way to Austria to stay with some friends, then, who knows? I'm spontaneous."

We continued to talk as we all slipped into our sleeping bags.

"I didn't think it got so cold here in autumn," Lyn said, trying to read her guidebook with the flashlight. "I'm freezing."

"You can always warm up beside me," said Mike. "Ladies, don't fight over me now."

Lyn and I laughed. Yeah, like we would resort to such desperation.

"I think we're good. We'll survive one night like this," I reassured Mike.

But the dark-haired guy was looking at me intently. I looked into his eyes. They reminded me of someone or some place.

Lesson: Experiencing life is a great way to learn and gain knowledge. You can't learn everything from a book.

Chapter 4

We woke to church bells ringing loudly. All of us stirred, and I sat up and glanced at my roommates. I had slept fitfully, thanks to the chilly autumn air and the unfamiliar territory. I hopped out of my sleeping bag and took out my toothbrush and other necessities. I headed outside while the others were taking their time. Lyn finally joined me outside.

"How did you sleep?" I asked.

"Not well. It was cold and I kept waking up."

I nodded.

Soon we could hear the guys talking on the other side of the building, which looked better in daylight than it had at dusk. Still, none of us was eager to repeat the experience.

We all got into the car, which I now reluctantly had to drive.

"You're brave to be driving here. I wouldn't want to do it," said Mike and John agreed.

"This is the last time until we leave, that's for sure." I started the car and off we went to the next hostel on our list.

We checked in and took showers. I happily washed off the grime of the night before. The hot water felt great and the change of clothes refreshing.

"What do you think of the guys?" I asked Lyn as we got dressed.

"Well, I think John likes you. He keeps staring at you, especially when you're not looking. I think Mike is nice. Just not my type. What do you think of them?"

"I feel I have a connection with John for some reason. I can't explain it. So we'll see."

"He's cute. He has a sweetness about him. Seems like a gentle kind of guy. Much better than the macho guys out there. Now they are a number."

John and Mike were waiting for us in the lobby to get breakfast and then go sightseeing. All of us looked much better than the day before. John stared at me as I walked in, then he offered me a smile. I returned it, and Lyn poked me as if to say she told me so.

After breakfast, we looked at our books to see which sites we'd visit in the next few days. Lots to cram in, but we had a rudimentary plan by the time we left the restaurant.

"I'm going to gain weight if I stay here," moaned Lyn. "These pastries are to die for." She patted her flat abdomen.

"Better than Holland or Belgium?" I asked. I remembered the yummy deserts and unbelievable chocolate.

"They're all good. Too good." She sighed.

John tapped my hand to get my attention. I

26

immediately felt warmth in my body. I glanced over at him and he said, "So where are you going after Paris?"

"Lyn and I are going to the coast of Spain, and then we split up in Cadiz. I'm not happy about that."

"Come to Africa with me then," said Lyn as she finished off her coffee.

"I haven't seen Europe, which is what I really came to do. Africa may have to be another trip."

I looked down at my hand. John still had his hand on top of it. When he saw me look at it, he pulled it away quickly. "Sorry," he said. "I didn't mean to take liberties with you."

I smiled. "No, that was alright." I didn't dare look at Lyn, who had always observed everything around her. Mike, who was engrossed in his maps and books, didn't seem to notice much of anything.

"So, we're off to the Louvre and then the Eiffel Tower," he said. "We should get going. I hear it takes hours and hours to see the Louvre."

Paris was like a romantic fire, lighting my heart. It made it glow brighter and brighter, until there was only a combustion of love everywhere. Paris melts me like no other city. That day, I realized that to know Paris is to love her. There was no area that romance and love wouldn't find you. And John and I were finding this to be especially true of us.

He had his arm around me on the train, and I didn't

object. "I thought you might be cold," he said.

"I'm not, but you can keep it there." I felt that familiar sense again. A feeling we'd done this many times before.

Lyn smirked at me, and Mike paid no attention at all. I could have been naked and he wouldn't have noticed.

The Louvre proved to be amazing. Rooms upon rooms of paintings. An overwhelming sense of visual stimuli overtook me. Bright colors and detailed images seared into my brain. The Mona Lisa painting looked so small, that it was almost out of place compared to the much larger paintings in the room. Yet the famous painting seemed to smile on us. Almost like she knew something we didn't. I wanted to know her secret, but I didn't have time to spend all day with her, or I might have discovered it.

As we roamed from room to room, I would declare one painting the best, only to discover one even better. It became our amusement as John and I looked at the paintings. We guessed what the artist was trying to say in each one. We laughed at some of our interpretations.

Sometimes Lyn and Mike wandered behind us, and other times in front of us. We always managed to find each other. A very good thing, since the Louvre seemed endless.

When we came out of the museum, John found a flowering yellow rose and picked it. He shyly gave it to me. "A rose for my own flower." I reached out and took it, then kissed him lightly.

"Okay, you two. What's going on?" Lyn asked.

"Nothing," I said. Now Mike actually looked up from his book.

"Is something going on between you two?" he said, finally noticing our togetherness.

"No. We really don't like each other," said John, smiling.

"Well, be careful about falling in love. Paris is a dangerous place for that."

By the time we reached the top of the Eiffel Tower, John and I couldn't keep our hands off each other. We kissed passionately and didn't care if anyone was watching us.

Paris opened my heart, but John was the one to take it. I'd never felt such an emotional connection to someone before. I couldn't explain it. Mystery, excitement, and fate swelled up in me. He touched my heart and soul.

"I think I have feelings for you," he whispered in the Tower, as he held me.

"I'm beginning to feel the same way about you. We hardly know each other, though," I whispered back.

"Or maybe we've known each other forever. You seem so familiar to me."

"I know what you mean." Paris made us drunk on love. That had to be it. Who falls in love so quickly in Paris? I'd have to find statistics on that one.

Later in the room at our hostel, Lyn started asking questions.

"So, I saw you two kissing madly in the Tower. How was it?"

"Very enjoyable." I remembered how my heart raced.

"So his tongue knows its way around your mouth. Good to know." We laughed.

"You're so funny. Do you think that it's fate that we met?"

"Absolutely. What are the chances that on our first day in Paris, you two meet? The stars aligned for that one. The behind-the-scenes maneuvering that took place. It's no accident." We got into our beds and went to sleep.

Lesson: Beware of strangers who turn out to be so much more.

Chapter 5

Soon John and I became inseparable, so it was no surprise to me when he and Mike asked if they could accompany Lyn and me to Spain. Naturally, I answered in the affirmative.

I knew the trip would take them slightly out of their way, but they didn't seem concerned about that.

My backpack had been stolen from the car, when I inadvertently left it in the back seat. It took a couple of days to replace my airline ticket and travelers checks. I'd bought a smaller backpack and Lyn helped me shop for some new clothes. I picked out clothes I knew would be appropriate for the trip. Traveling light was the way to go. The theft had been a blessing in disguise.

I looked at the car and patted it on the hood. "Be good and take us to Spain in one piece." Everyone offered to drive, but I liked driving on the freeways. We wanted a smaller town, so we picked Sitges, near Barcelona, after reading all the reviews in our books. We planned to spend four or five days there, and then all of us would go our separate ways. But John and I had other ideas, which we had discussed a day earlier.

"You can come to Austria and stay with me there. How about that? I can't lose you now after we just found each other," he'd said as we sipped wine outside a French café.

"You'd think we'd been looking for each other for years," I replied. "I can travel to Austria. I don't know about staying with your friends, but we'll see."

"I never thought I'd want someone so much until I met you. But we're still at the beginning stages."

"I'm not rushing. I want to take this nice and slow," I reassured him. "This might not work out at all. So we'll see." I took a sip of my wine. John put his hand on my other hand from across the table. I felt a warmth creep into my body. I loved his touch.

"I think this is the real thing. I've never felt like this before. It's like I've known you for years already."

"Strange. Me too." We looked into each other's eyes and I saw how deep his were. But I'd been burned once already, and wasn't about to get fooled again. Still, there was sincerity about his face and eyes, like he meant what he said.

We arrived in Sitges, which appeared nearly deserted due to the off-season. A few hotels and stores were open, as was the nightclub that would become our nightly pastime. Lyn and I rented a room, and the guys rented another one. The price was very low for such a nice hotel. We knew prices would be outrageous in the spring and summer.

While Lyn and I unpacked she said, "He's in love with

you. I'm sure of it." She grinned at me, like she knew a secret.

"It's too soon. We've only known each other a week or so."

"He's got goo-goo eyes for you. His puppy dog look follows you everywhere you go. It's hilarious."

"He does not." Secretly it was nice to get confirmation of something I suspected.

"You're in love, too. But you're too stubborn to admit it. Like that song by 10cc "I'm Not in Love." You know the one where the guy is in denial that he is in love."

"I like that song, even if it's older. But I don't know if I'm in love yet."

That night, John serenaded me under our hotel window with that *exact* song.

I listened to John singing the words and grimaced, as he sang off key at times. I turned abruptly to Lyn and said, "Did you put him up to this?" She was lying on the bed laughing hysterically. I threw my pillow at her. She ducked and rolled off her bed, still giggling.

I didn't know what to believe as I walked outside to meet John. I kissed him and thanked him for the song. I was glad there were no other patrons in the hotel to witness the spectacle.

"The song is not true. I'm in love with you and I wanted to share it with you," he said quietly.

"I'm in love too, but I'm still going slowly on this.

After all, we're parting ways soon."

"Lyn and Mike already know. In fact Mike's been kidding me about it all day."

"I wonder if those two are talking about us," I thought out loud. "Oh well, I guess there's nothing I can do about it."

"You are going to visit me in Austria after the Canary Islands, right? Why are you going there?"

"For some sun before hitting colder weather and snow. Hopefully I'll have a tan next time you see me."

"I'm going to miss you. I need you to promise you'll meet me in Austria."

"I promise. I swear. But I don't know how long I'll be in the Islands, and then there's the journey to Austria. Could be several weeks."

He held me tight and whispered, "Just come back to me. That's all I want. Or I'll have to try to find you. And don't think I can't." He kissed me again.

"You have my word." I looked up at the windows to see Lyn and Mike out on their respective balconies, watching us.

"Don't you two have better things to do?" I shouted up at them.

"No. You two are too much fun to watch," Mike shouted back. Lyn just laughed.

John and I kissed each other goodnight. And that was the night my dream came back to haunt me.

As I jumped from the plane with my parachute in place, I felt excitement and fear at the same time. I was falling quickly towards the earth. It was exhilarating and I felt so free. Then the parachute opened, and I slowly descended to a grassy spot. Then I quickly looked up to see another skydiver falling fast. Too fast. The chute wasn't opening. I stood in horror as I watched him fall and hit the ground, dead. I screamed. People rushed over to console me. The skydiver was my husband.

I'd had dreams of death several times that ended up coming true, but this one hit too close to home. This was my husband, who would die before his time. And I would be left a widow. I did not like that idea. I didn't think there was anything I could do about changing the fate of that event. Aunt Emma couldn't advise me. She claimed there were choices involved.

And no matter how many times I had the dream or analyzed it, it always ended the same. What was the message of the dream? Life is short, so enjoy it? Or just beware, your dreams come true? Being forewarned is a blessing in disguise?

I decided to put the dream out of my mind and live my life. There was nothing else to do. I couldn't let it paralyze everything I did. I would let it play out like karma and fate wanted, and would prepare as best I could for it, hoping it wouldn't happen.

Lesson: Bad dreams can come true just as easily as

Twist of Fate

good ones.

Chapter 6

Traveling together means you learn lots of facts and traits about each other fairly quickly. It's a double-edged sword. John and I knew things about each other that might have taken months to learn, under different circumstances. I knew he had dreams of wanting to play in a band, but didn't think he was good enough. He liked working in a music store more than working on boats like his dad. His mother taught piano part-time. They were a middle class family and he had no siblings. Neither of us had a very religious upbringing. I enjoyed my friend's various churches, but none of them clicked for me. Too traditional. Same with John. He got bored and restless easily, like me. But John's lack of direction seemed off-putting at times. He seemed to live for today and not care about tomorrow. I was the opposite. He never told me why he had decided to travel. He'd just made up his mind one day and that was it. I knew there was a secret there that he might eventually share. He seemed to have an artist's heart and soul. And as much as I knew of our differences, I knew deep down that we had a soul connection of some sort. Soul mates even.

When I looked into his eyes, I saw my own soul. And it was beautiful. I was home. And he told me that he felt the same way.

Sadly, we still had to say goodbye. I felt a deep sense of dread as I drove Mike and John to the train station to catch a train to Austria. Everyone was eerily quiet in the car. Sitges had been a great stop for us, and we all promised to return one day.

John's goodbye left me with a feeling of emptiness, even though we knew we'd see each other again. Or would we? Events can change quickly when you travel.

Our mood was melancholy as we waited on the platform. Train stations are full of arrivals and departing scenes, where hellos are just as frequent as goodbyes. But this was no hello. John looked even more dejected after we said goodbye. I felt a sadness that I couldn't explain. Lyn kissed John on the cheek and whispered in his ear. He grinned. We hugged Mike, and hoped we'd see him again. We had addresses and phone numbers.

I watched them board the train. John was still carrying his guitar, which he now regretted bringing, since it was just one more thing to carry.

As the train pulled out, we waved one last time. Moments like these are precious, even though they don't last long.

"What did you say to John?" I asked Lyn as we headed for the car.

"Oh. I said you two were meant for each other. True?"

"Probably."

"And you say *he's* wishy-washy." We both chuckled.

"On to Cadiz, where *we* part ways," Lyn reminded me.

"Today is a day of goodbyes." I said, feeling sadder by the minute. "How long are you staying in Cadiz?"

"A few days, and then along the coast for a bit before Africa. We must stay in touch. Promise me that."

"I promise. And you too."

When we got to Cadiz, I dropped Lyn off at a hotel, and it felt like we hugged forever.

"I'm going to miss you. You're so great to travel with," I said.

"Me too. You must write and let me know about this love affair. I'm curious. And don't forget to be true to yourself. That's important."

"I will."

I found an agent and bought my ticket. I was pleasantly surprised to find that Cadiz was a quaint seaside town. I instantly knew I wanted to spend more time here at a later date.

I looked at the ferry and was surprised how large and nice it looked. Like a miniature cruise ship. The bottom deck was filling with many vehicles. As I boarded the ship, I showed my ticket to a young Spanish man named Henri. He was about five-foot-five, with dark hair and eyes. Not a bad-looking fellow. He looked professional in his white uniform. He took a liking to me, and asked me to meet him in the dance club that evening. I told him I didn't know if I would be there or not. He escorted me to my quarters.

Well, what a surprise! My private cabin had two single beds and a bunk bed. Henri then said goodbye, reminded me about dancing, and left. I picked a single bed near the bunk. As I unpacked, an Australian woman came in.

"I'm Sue," she said, "I'll take the other single bed."

As she unpacked, I introduced myself and gave a brief history.

"I hope we don't get seasick. The waves can be really rough sometimes," she said as she bit into an apple.

"I hope not. I've never been seasick."

"Don't worry. There's a doctor on board. Second floor, I think. And we're on the third." She explained how she and her husband were catching a ship for South Africa, where they were moving. They saved money by staying in dorm-like facilities like this cabin. It seemed like a lot of English and Australian residents were immigrating to South Africa. A mass exodus I had never heard about.

"Let's go check out the Rock of Gibraltar," Sue said. "We'll be passing it soon after we leave port."

Nodding, I grabbed my camera and followed her out of the cabin.

Soon the decks were filled with people, and before I knew it, we glided away. People waved at their loved ones. I noticed Lyn on the dock, waving goodbye to me. I was touched that she'd come to see me off. I waved goodbye. And we shouted we'd keep in touch. Soon she was nothing but a speck in the distance.

Eventually the ship sailed near the Rock of Gibraltar. The massive, dark rock jutted out of the water as if daring anyone to mess with it. It was an amazing sight for sure, so I snapped photo after photo. I wondered what stories it would tell me, if I dared sit on it and breathe in its essence.

I watched until the Rock was out of sight, getting smaller and smaller. Then our boat started rocking some and I headed for my cabin. I smelled diesel fumes that almost made me gag. I looked at the culprit to see the ship's funnels blowing out dark smoke. I became nauseated and made a quick dash to my room. I vomited in the toilet, but didn't feel much better, so I lay down. I looked over at the bunk bed to see backpacks on them, but no owners.

My stomach was still queasy and the ship rocked even worse than before. It was too late to get off the boat, or I would have. I didn't remember signing up for this. It was past dinner when my two Spanish roommates came in. We introduced ourselves, then they kept to themselves. Sue showed up and offered me some coconut for my stomach, then left again. Shortly after, I vomited that up as well. Lying down seemed to be the only thing that would help. I decided to sleep. During the night, my Spanish roommates got sick as well. Fun times. Sue never complained of nausea the whole trip.

The next day when I saw Henri, he was annoyed at

me for not going dancing. I explained my situation, but I didn't get much sympathy. He went with me to find the doctor, who had banker's hours. I wondered why the doctor even bothered being here. I found tea, soft drinks, and water in machines. Somehow I kept missing the dining room hours. I couldn't get fresh air because there wasn't any. The diesel smell permeated everywhere. It only made me sicker to my stomach. I still faced another day and night of this misery. I realized that the bed would be my salvation. And by noon my roommates were in the same condition as me, staying in their beds. We took turns using the restroom. We could have used another one for sure. I couldn't eat a thing, and even fluids wouldn't stay down. This sickness had overpowered and totally humbled me. I had nothing to compare it to. It was a first.

The second day at sea still did not bring relief. I was determined to eat, though, and found the dining room open at noon. Feeling famished, I opted for all sorts of foods, but immediately realized the smell of it made me nauseated. A man sitting near me noticed my discomfort and offered some pills for my stomach. I gladly accepted them, thinking they might kill me, which at this point would be a welcome relief. I took one, not knowing what they were, then grabbed some fruit with me and headed for the inside stairwell. Down and down I went.

Soon I noticed I was in the vehicle storage area. I became ill so I looked for a restroom. A good-looking

Spanish worker came over to help me. He saw me patting my abdominal area and nodded like he understood. Under normal circumstances, I might have been worried or even a little afraid, but the caring look in his eyes told me he could be trusted. He took my arm and guided me to the restroom about eight feet away. He came in with me and suddenly, before I could enter the toilet, he'd taken me in his arms and kissed me. His tongue thrust into my mouth, and I gagged. I opened the toilet door and vomited into it. He held me while I did this and kept my long hair out of my face. When I was done, I went to the sink and rinsed out my mouth. The man then gently took my arm and guided me to the stairs, and to my cabin. I thanked him. I was too sick to be kissed and wondered what he had been thinking. Maybe he just didn't understand how sick I really was. I never saw him again, but I would *never* forget the incident.

In the room, I looked in the mirror and was shocked at my appearance. My face now had a green-grey look to it. I'd never looked so ghastly in my life.

Lesson: Be wary of Spanish men in restrooms. And be prepared for boat rides.

43

Chapter 7

We finally arrived on sweet land at eight the next morning. If I hadn't been so sick, I might have kissed it. I had tried to say goodbye to Henri as I disembarked, but he angrily turned away from me. Too many no-shows had put him off. Oh well. I now had some pills to help me, even though I didn't need them anymore. As I walked on wobbly legs to the town of Las Palmas, I overheard conversations of how sick many people were on the boat. Some claimed it had been the worst, especially the diesel smell. I would never be able to smell it again without feeling nauseated.

At the hotel, I checked into my room and looked again at my face and body. I'd lost weight and my face still looked green. It would take several days to recover, and I still faced taking a ferry back. This time I planned to be better prepared. So for the next few days, I walked on the beach, ate and drank well, and took care of myself. I knew I wouldn't get much of a tan but just smelling the fresh sea air helped. The weather was not as hot as I thought it would be, but reminded me of springtime. Even though there were sights to see, I was in no mood or condition to look at them. I wanted to be in a better state of health and mind before venturing anywhere. My whole equilibrium and psyche had been thrown off.

Finally, I looked in the mirror one day to see a reflection I recognized. My skin had turned pink again; my eyes looked brighter and not drab. My state of mind wasn't so dull. I went into the town to explore, and to check into flight options to Cadiz.

"You don't want to fly. It's too expensive," said the Spanish woman behind the desk. "You should take the ferry. It's much, much cheaper."

"I did. I got sick. I'd like to fly. What is the price?" I was determined to fly this time. As long as it didn't cost an outrageous amount.

"It's like three-hundred dollars with the exchange rate. It's expensive. Do you still want it?" she asked, looking up at me for confirmation.

"That's ridiculous! The ferry is only forty or fifty!" I finally relented and talked over my options with her. I felt better and just wanted to see Europe and John sooner.

"Okay. I have one for you. And it's even cheaper than the other ferries."

"Why is it cheaper?"

"Day of the week or type of boat. But it leaves the day you want."

I paid her for my place on the boat and walked to the drugstore in search of Dramamine. I bought postcards and realized how much I missed John. I'd been too sick to care about him or anyone else before. It would have been great if he had been with me. Of course, he might have also gotten sick, which wouldn't have been much fun.

I hated being sick. It made me feel weak and helpless, so I prepared for the worst ship crossing possible. I bought plenty of food and drinks. I would probably end up in bed for the whole journey. And it was just as well, because as I looked out from the marina to check out the boat, all I saw was a freighter.

Lesson: Life is full of surprises, that's why it can be helpful to have low expectations.

Chapter 8

"There must be some mistake." I spoke to the crew standing near the ship. "Is this the boat to Cadiz?"

"Yes. Cadiz. Today," said one of the workers as he prepared to load containers onto the boat. I'd been had by the agent. No wonder the ticket was so cheap! I looked around for something to do for the next several hours, and finally headed to the restaurant nearby.

I sat down and noticed a blond haired, good looking man sitting nearby. We smiled and he came over to join me.

We introduced ourselves. His name was Connor and he had a British accent.

We ate and talked for hours about our travels and dreams. He was so nice and I realized I could easily fall for someone like him. We enjoyed each other's company, and soon it was time to embark on the boat. A part of me didn't want to leave. Connor wanted me to stay for a few days and then travel with him. He was traveling to Europe and then Asia. He seemed well-to-do. I suddenly found myself questioning what I owed John and, at what point does one relationship take precedent over another? I could easily ditch John and be with the Connor, and what did that say about me? I felt connected with John, but did that make him the right guy? Would there always be someone better? Or worse? I thought I loved John, but was that true? Maybe I was just in love with Paris and the romantic air that I got caught up in. Sitges had been fun and wonderful. After several minutes of debating myself, I knew. I could never hurt someone or break my promises. My word was as good as gold.

We exchanged addresses and phone numbers, then I got up and kissed him goodbye. He said he wished I would stay, and a part of me did, too. I would always look back on this day and wonder whether I made the right decision.

The huge black and red boat before me did not look inviting at all. Not a people boat. I felt like a stowaway as I climbed down the steps below the deck. My cabin was small and had its own restroom. I even had a porthole. My own room. If I got sick, at least that would make the trip worthwhile.

I headed upstairs to explore the deck. I watched the crew work for a while. A few plastic chairs had been set out, and I sat there for a bit. A young Australian man joined me and introduced himself as Jim; he was heading back home.

"I didn't know we'd be on a freighter, did you?" I asked as I watched the crew.

"No. Sometimes it happens. Don't you love traveling? A new experience every day."

I told him about my seasickness.

"This boat shouldn't be as rough, and the winds are blowing in the other direction. Should be fine." He then stood up to wave to a woman with long dark hair on the marina. He explained that he'd been staying with her, but now he had to leave. "Other responsibilities." He didn't elaborate, and I didn't ask. I looked again and there was Connor waving to me. I explained who he was to Jim.

"He seems like a pleasant guy. And you don't want him?"

"He's nice. I have someone else right now that I made a promise to."

"Be careful about those promises. Sometimes you can't keep them. Doesn't make you a bad person. Just a person who makes mistakes. We're only human."

"Well I can't just leave someone I made a promise to. That wouldn't be right."

"Right for who? You're not married to the guy, right? Are you engaged?"

"No, but still."

"So what's your problem? You have no commitment to this other person. None. And yet you're giving up a perfectly good man for another. We do it all the time. It's called choice. Even freedom."

"It doesn't seem morally right to me. I gave my word. What use am I without that? No one would trust me if I backed out. And John would be left wondering what happened to me. I would feel guilty about what I did. I don't even know if I could be happy knowing I had done that to someone."

"Who cares?" said my new guru.

"I guess *I* do. I have to live with myself. I wouldn't be able to look at myself in the mirror without hating what I saw. Wondering if I made the right decision."

"Now we're getting somewhere. Good. You know yourself. Always be true to who you are. Don't let anyone tell you otherwise. But that doesn't mean you can't have male friends." He winked at me.

I continued to watch Connor and the dark haired gal wave to us as we sailed away. Soon they were tiny dots. Now I hoped I'd made the right choice.

The journey was smoother this time. I had food, water, and pills. I only felt nauseated a few times. Jim and I shared food and conversation on the deck. The diesel smell was only barely there. A welcome change from the last journey.

I felt one hundred percent better by the time I set foot in Cadiz. I was looking forward to being with John. At least that's what I kept telling myself.

Lesson: There are no right or wrong decisions. Only consequences. And those can get you killed.

Chapter 9

I decided to hitchhike across Spain and France to Venice. I had read about many women doing this and I had to try it, no matter how apprehensive I might be. I'd been going outside my comfort zone this whole trip, and this would be another challenge, as well as a test of courage. I realized I liked learning about myself. Until I saw the police car pull up beside me.

An Italian policeman rolled down his window to talk to me.

"You can't hitchhike on the Autostrade," he said in nearly perfect English, referring to the freeway I was standing on.

"This is where I got dropped off by a man who had to exit here. I had no choice," I explained.

"Well, get in." the officer said. "We can take you to the garage up the road and you should be able to get a ride from someone there. Just don't do this again," he scolded.

I hopped into the backseat of the police car and they headed off to the garage. Along the way we chatted about the differences between America and Italy. A few minutes later we pulled up in front of the garage. I thanked them as I got out. There was a café next to the garage, and a young man with a backpack watched me.

"What happened?" he asked me.

I told him.

"You're lucky. They could have fined you, or worse, taken you to jail."

"I'm glad that didn't happen. Where are you going?"

"I'm off to Geneva with the couple inside. I'm sure they'd give you a lift near Venice." The couple agreed and I hopped into the back of the panel van with this new acquaintance. We couldn't see much scenery from the van, so after talking some, we both fell asleep.

The couple dropped me off in Milan, then I ended up taking a train to Venice. The train rolled into the station and I noticed water on both sides of it. Water, water everywhere. That was the welcoming sign of Venice. As soon as I left the train, the stench of the canals invaded my nostrils. I sniffed the air as I tried to place the odors, but there were too many.

"Mainly garbage, pollution, and mildew," said an Italian woman walking beside me. "You'll get used to it." She strode past me, wheeling her suitcase.

According to my guidebook, I had two choices: take a water taxi or walk to my hotel. I decided to walk to get the lay of the land, but soon discovered my usual lack of direction was even worse here. I meandered from one alleyway and bridge to the next, merely to find I'd gone in the wrong direction. Total frustration filled my body, when a young girl of seven showed up and guided me to the hotel. She was thin with long, dark hair and an infectious smile. She didn't speak much English but understood my map. I gave her some money for her help, and watched as she gleefully skipped away from me. As usual, Europeans, young and old, seemed more than willing to help out strangers in need.

After checking in, I decided to explore this unique city. I noticed boats of every kind carrying residents and visitors to and fro. I then stared at the famous gondolas rocking on the waves, and wished John was here. There was so much romance surrounding me, and I was by myself. Then it happened. A sense of loneliness started to permeate my being, no matter how charming and beautiful the place. I wanted to shrug off the emptiness, but too many gondolas made it impossible to forget.

Hoping to overcome the feeling, I took myself on a tour of all the famous spots, and realized how photos never seemed to capture the true essence of them. Lone men gravitated towards me, wanting company. I was polite, but brushed most of them off. Traveling solo—especially for females—is an adventure in itself.

I took in the stunning architecture, trying to detach from the gloominess inside me. The overcast skies matched my mood, as I yearned for the sun. I loved Piazza San Marco, which appeared to be the heart and soul of Venice. It clearly served as a gathering place for residents and visitors alike. Crowds flocked here to exchange stories, see the sights, or just people watch. Italians spoke loudly and gestured frequently to stress their points of view. I soon found myself smiling at conversations I did not understand.

That night, looking at the deserted waterways and streets, sadness and depression overcame me. I felt more alone than I'd ever been in my life. This beautiful city of romance had become a city of despair. I vowed I would never return to Venice alone.

The next day, as much as I wanted to leave Venice, I made arrangements to spend several more days. I wanted to make the most of my time here. Then I called John in Salzburg.

"Hello?" It seemed like forever since I last heard his voice. I missed him and hoped he still wanted me to be with him. A lot can change in a short time when you're traveling.

"Hi John. It's Shawna. It's great to hear your voice. I'm letting you know that I'm in Venice and will be in Salzburg Friday. I hope that that's still okay." I waited to hear what he had to say before pouring my heart out to him. I needn't have worried.

"That's great, Shawna. I can't wait to see you. I miss you so much and think about you all the time. How's Venice? I've always wanted to see it. I received your postcards and letter."

"Good. Venice is romantic and you're not here. But

I'm going to enjoy it anyway. I miss you and wish you were here."

"Of course. I wish I were there with you. Maybe we can head down that way later. I really do miss you though. I thought you might not come back and had forgotten about me."

"I keep my promises." I didn't tell John about Connor. Not yet.

"Trust is important. I can't wait to see you."

"Me too. We have lots of catching up to do."

"I love you."

"I love you too." When I hung up the phone, I told myself I really meant it.

Lesson: Live in the moment, and enjoy it. You may never pass this way again.

Chapter 10

John greeted me at the Salzburg station, although I wasn't expecting him to be there. He smiled warmly and walked over quickly to greet me. We kissed and hugged. I had been anxious about whether I would feel the same way about him as when I last saw him. I did.

"I love the mountains and the snow. It's not as cold as I thought it would be," I said with wide eyes as I pointed to the mountains outside the train station. We held hands as we walked.

"Well, I'll always keep you warm. You know that." I nodded.

We walked to a hotel I'd picked out, since I didn't want to stay with his friends. John moved in with me after several days. I had a feeling our time together would be more intimate this time. And I was right. Our intimacy took on a new meaning, as we finally made a sexual connection. There seemed to be a spiritual connection that neither of us expected. He touched an inner part of me, as if he was caressing my soul. Our insides danced with one another to different beats from a tango to a waltz, which caused our heart and souls to become one. I had an orgasm of love that brought me closer to divinity that I never felt before. Our spiritual essences meshed, and I couldn't tell where I began or ended. It went on forever. Although I had no words to describe what I was feeling, John put his own words to it.

"I feel a connection to something greater than us when we make love. It's amazing and blows me away. I never knew sex could feel like that. It's never happened before," he said after one of our many liaisons.

"It feels other worldly and I'm grateful. So grateful." I wondered if I could ever feel this way with other men. After several weeks we were on the move again.

"We have to pack and get ready for our trip to Greece. The orange picking season doesn't last forever. It starts in December and ends around March." John reminded me, as I dressed. "I like your body. It's small, but strong."

"I like yours, too. Especially your hairy chest." I wanted to touch him, but knew we needed to get moving and start hitchhiking to Greece. We would miss Bavaria, with its chestnuts roasting outside and the snow, but we'd already spent a month here sightseeing in Switzerland and Germany. We would hitchhike through Austria and Yugoslavia before arriving in Greece.

As it turned out, though, the best ride was with an Austrian family headed to Italy. From Italy, a wonderful Yugoslavian man named Duro, picked us up and took us back to his place in Belgrade. We spent the night sleeping on one end of his sofa, while he slept on the other end. We were grateful to him for the hospitality, even though it wasn't an ideal situation.

In the morning, he made us breakfast and introduced us to his friends who had come by to visit. We wished we could have stayed longer, as we felt these were the most welcoming people we had met so far. Europe just kept getting better and better.

By now I'd been traveling four months, but it felt like a year. Towns, cities, and people, came in and out of our lives. We needed to stay longer to really get the full experience, but for John, money had become an issue. We needed to work if we wanted to stay in Europe.

After being picked up in Yugoslavia by a truck driver, we finally arrived in Athens. As I looked out over the shimmering whiteness of the city, I felt like I was in another place and time. From the high road leading into town, I felt nostalgia creeping into my body. Another familiar place that felt like home. This one held more mystery for me, and I wondered what Greece had in store for us. Would Athens be a positive or negative experience?

As we dropped off our belongings in the hotel, we noticed a blood drive going on. Since they were paying for this service, John and I volunteered.

"I can only use one of you," explained the Greek man running the drive. He nodded to John and then turned to me. "You have a problem. You're anemic. Have you had this before?" he asked.

"No. I gave blood before leaving for Europe, but that

was months ago. I should be fine, although that might explain my tiredness."

"You need iron. So buy a multivitamin and mineral combination. Travelers don't eat as healthy as they should." I watched as he prepped John, and extracted a liter of blood. Then after he got paid, we headed for the pharmacy.

While browsing for vitamins, I saw what looked like birth control pills on the rack. I took a second look. I asked the clerk who confirmed this. I was surprised they were sold over the counter.

"I'm getting several of these," I said happily to John. I pulled down four of them. John smiled.

"Don't get too carried away," he said. "But I understand. You can't buy them over the counter in England either. So backwards."

"Now we won't have to use the other things." I motioned to the condom aisle. I'd found treasure in Greece. Who knew?

"Yes. I'm okay using them. But this is better," John agreed.

I ended up with a six-month supply, thinking it would last until I got home. I bought some vitamins and minerals with iron. Greece was quickly moving up to first place in our jaunt around Europe.

We climbed up to the Acropolis and sat on the marble pillars and steps. A sense of wonderment came over me, as to how this gorgeous structure could have been built so long ago. The marble was hard and heavy. The atmosphere was so full of life and timeless, I half expected Socrates and Plato to show up and explain their philosophies to us. But alas, none showed up at that time. We stared down at the city of Athens below us. What a magnificent view. The water in the background gave it a postcard look.

"This place is amazing," said John as we turned back to the Acropolis.

"I love it. I want to come back here someday. Maybe we could live in Athens." I said as I looked at all the grand columns and architecture.

"You say that about almost every place. Just pick one," he joked.

"I can't. They all hold my interests. I could spend eternity just exploring Europe."

"Well, I would like to go to Nepal and Tibet someday. Wouldn't you?" John and I now sat on the steps.

"Absolutely. Once I get my iron levels up."

I turned to look at the Acropolis one last time before leaving. I hoped it would stand for hundreds more years.

I had a dream that night. A philosopher resembling Socrates came to visit. We sat and talked outside the Acropolis.

"It's a tragedy to be here on Earth. A Greek tragedy, I tell you," I said to him as we looked into each other's eyes.

"*You never wanted to come back here. You have to discover why you did.*"

"*Am I being punished?*"

"*Not at all. You chose it,*" he said, fingering his long beard.

"*Not a wise decision,*" I answered.

"*That remains to be seen. You're young, and you have lots of adventures ahead of you.*"

"*What advice do you have for me?*" He touched my arm gently, but his stare was intense.

"*Don't forget where you really come from. It's most important. For now, enjoy your travels. A gift you gave to yourself. John came along for the ride. A freeloader, if you will. But there's more to this than meets the eye. Laugh often. The Gods do.*" After he finished speaking, he disappeared.

The next morning, as we were lying in bed, I told John about my dream. He thought it was interesting, but he had his own dream to consider. He told me that he frequently dreams he's falling down a mountain. He can't seem to get out of the free fall.

"Do you die?" I asked.

"I'm not sure. I wake up before I land. It's strange. I've had this dream for some time. It always ends the same way."

"Yes. That's a strange one." I decide to not tell John about my skydiving dream, and I wonder if I ever will.

Lesson: Dreams have messages and it's best we pay attention to them.

Chapter 11

I stared at the ferry with uneasiness. Although not a long ride to Crete, I remembered my seasickness from two and a half months ago.

"It should be fine," John said as we climbed aboard. "The locals say it's not such a rough ride." We'd been assured that we could find jobs in Crete to pick oranges or olives. But I wasn't convinced I wouldn't get seasick again. It had been a most unpleasant experience. "Listen, Sunbeam, you'll be fine. No need to worry," John said as he put him arm around me.

"I know that nickname is sarcastic sometimes, but I'm still okay with it." I said. John fluctuated between Sunbeam and Sunshine. It'd been like that since Spain. "What should I call you?"

"What do you *want* to call me? I can think of lots of names."

"I'll just call you Moonbeam. How's that?"

"Why? It seems like we should probably switch them."

"You started it by calling me Sunshine," I replied with a smirk, "You cast the first stone. If you don't like Moonbeam, I'll call you Moon for short. I think it suits you, right? You're dreamy and intuitive."

"Just like you," he answered immediately. "But I think

I'll be okay with it. As long as you never say it in public."

"Fine. Besides, we're both water signs. I can't believe our birthdays are so close together. That's very odd. Too much alike, maybe?" I wondered how long it had been since I'd had an astrology chart done. It had been a long time.

"In some ways, but I think love overcomes all. I really do." He stroked my hands as he spoke. Then he lifted my hand to his lips and kissed it.

"Spoken like a true romantic. And you say you're not like the moon?" I said, laughing. John joined me.

"So we have about three months of working in Crete," he said. "That's a long time for us to be in one place. We'll be done sometime in March, and then we'll go on to the Middle East." John continued to hold my hand as we walked along the deck. We watched the lights of Athens get further and further away.

"I don't know what it will be like. I just know we both need to make more money. I'm not ready to go back home yet. Are you?" John looked uneasy now. There was silence for several minutes before he continued.

"I should have told you before. I broke up with this woman before I left. She gave me a hard time about it and harassed me. I finally had to get far away. She was stalking me and saying mean things about me behind my back. It was a terrible breakup, and I don't want to go through that again." He gave me a gentle look. "Please don't ever do that to me."

"Well, I wouldn't. I don't chase after men." I said, relieved that John hadn't done any criminal activity. My ex-finance had a brother who was involved in gang activity; he would have killed someone without a second thought. Although Sam was not like his brother, I had been secretly glad that I had broken up with him. I had told John about this shortly after I'd met him.

"What's her name? What happened?" I asked. I was finally getting some answers.

"Natalie. She played in a band with my friends, Jackie and Roger. I knew her for about six months. When I realized she wanted to control my life I knew I had to leave." He looked intently at me, and seemed relieved to talk about it.

"So she was a control freak? Maybe possessive? Is that right? I wanted to get the whole picture of what happened."

"Sort of. I just couldn't do anything right. She was on my case about everything. After we broke up, she wouldn't leave me alone. I just felt trapped and this trip was my escape. I didn't plan on meeting anyone. That just happened. But I'm glad it did." He leaned over and kissed me softly.

"Me too. But I'm a rebound for you. Maybe we should wait before getting so involved. I mean, are you really over her?" I looked into his eyes for answers. I knew that if this relationship wasn't totally finished, it would bleed into the next one. I wanted none of that.

"Yeah. She means nothing to me. And I needed a break from London. Just for a time. It's not permanent." He looked back at me lovingly. His eyes always did a number on me.

We kissed, and as he pulled away, I watched the moonlight bouncing off the water and illuminating John's face. It gave his features an almost angelic look.

"You look like an angel in this light," he said to me.

"I was thinking the same about you."

I hugged him. The boat hardly swayed much at all. The Mediterranean waters were calm as we stretched our sleeping bags on the deck for the night.

The next morning we asked around, and found an owner of several orange groves looking for cheap labor. His name was Yanni, and he offered us a flat rate of seven dollars apiece. We told him we could accept that; now we just had to find a cheap place to live. A few miles away, we found a small town near Hania and decided to hang out.

We walked around the town for a bit and finally found the only café.

"This café only has men in it. Why is that?" I asked John as we ordered food and tea. All the men stared at us as we sat down. Strangers in a small town. Obviously we were now a source of gossip for them.

"I guess Greek women don't hang out in cafes. There

are a couple over there." He nodded to the back of the café. I glanced over and saw them.

Before we knew it, a few glasses of ouzo came our way. Compliments of the locals. We thanked them for their hospitality. Greek people were always buying us food and drinks, but no one had been kinder to us than the Yugoslavians.

An English woman named Maggie showed up and started conversing with us. When we told her about our job at the groves, she explained that she would be working there too. She had heard of an abandoned police station building not far from the café, and did not want to squat in it by herself. Would we be interested in joining her? She'd been in town several weeks and was dating one of the local men, Georges, but wouldn't live with him. That was understandable in this small town. Locals did not want foreign women dating their Greek men, or vice versa.

"We can look at it after you eat," she said. "But it'd be nice to stay in a place that we wouldn't have to pay for. Save our money. I need to travel more after Greece."

She had long blonde hair and delicate features. She was dressed in jeans and a sweater with a rain jacket over her clothes. Our light coloring looked out of place with all the dark hair and olive skin.

"It wouldn't hurt to look. Shawna, what do you think?" John asked as he gulped his ouzo. The drink didn't seem to bother him, but he winced once.

"I'm game. It'd be nice to save most of our money." I sipped the ouzo, and made a face, then coughed. It burned all the way down my throat, and then my body felt very warm. The local men sitting nearby laughed as they watched us.

"You'll get used to it. It's a favorite drink around here," said Maggie. She sat with us and drank her tea. I offered her the last shot of ouzo, and she gulped it down like it was water.

After dinner we sauntered over to the building, which sat on the border of the large football field. It was a block building painted green and white. The windows were intact, and it looked like it hadn't been abandoned too long ago. As we got closer, we noticed that two people had just come out. They'd turned out to be a Canadian couple named Jean and Kyle, who said they'd gotten the clear from the locals to live in it. They welcomed us to join them. Jean had short brown hair and Kyle had red hair. Both had average builds and looked about our age. Jean would be picking oranges with us and Kyle worked on a different farm. He had lucked out with a driving job.

"Come on in and we'll show you around," said Kyle, gesturing to us with a smile on his face. Jean smiled as well. "I'm glad we won't be living here by ourselves. It's safe, but there's something weird about it."

As we climbed the five steps to the porch, an eerie feeling came over me. We stepped inside and slowly examined the place. Prison bars covered three of the rooms, and I joked that they were a welcoming sight. We turned left into a large open area with a fireplace and an old-fashioned chandelier hanging from the ceiling. There was no furniture, of course. We walked to the back and there stood the remnants of the kitchen. Large cement countertops, a sink with running water, a hollowed out fire pit on the countertop for cooking, and no fridge. To the right was a room with no windows. There was a back door in the kitchen and a large window.

"Jean and I took one of the front rooms as our bedroom, so you guys can have what you want."

John headed for the seclusion room, and Maggie headed to the front.

"What do you think?" he asked, walking inside and examining it.

"I don't like it. There are no windows and it's small. Besides I'm claustrophobic. Let's pick another room," I said quickly.

"Hear me out first. We can keep the door open all the time. We have privacy away from the others, and we get morning light from the window to wake us up for work. What do you think?"

"I'll give it a try, but I'm not guaranteeing anything. This room actually gives me the creeps. But the ones with bars aren't appealing either." Still, after a while I relented.

"And of course the toilet and shower don't work, so

we're stuck with the great outdoors. I know how much you love that," John said, softly poking my shoulder and teasing me.

"Yes, what woman wouldn't? It's the bathroom of my dreams." I rolled my eyes. "But the price is right."

"Our new roommates seem okay," John remarked, putting his pack in the room.

"Well, the ones we can see, anyway." John didn't seem to notice what I said as he unrolled his sleeping bag. I felt the ghosts of yesteryear crawling along the walls. I sensed their light presence, even though I couldn't see them. At least, not yet. I looked out the window to a spot that bothered me. I don't know why, but I shuddered. It was trying to tell me something. I figured one day I would know.

Lesson: Ghosts from past relationships live inside our minds and hearts. Our job is to resolve them completely or they will never go away.

Chapter 12

All of us made beds out of orange crates tied together. We placed cardboard on top of them, and then used our sleeping bags on top of that. It wasn't the most comfortable arrangement, but we got used to it. I stretched to loosen my back, wondering how long a body could last on something like this before real damage was done.

Our day began at seven thirty, and ended at four or five, depending on the whims of the owner and our keepers, as I lovingly called the boss man's uncle and various Greek locals working for him. Obviously we were the migrants who worked for peanuts, and were happy to do so. I always liked physical labor, even if it was tedious. I felt some stretching and exercise were always helpful if nothing else. John didn't agree.

"I don't know how long I can handle this," he moaned several days later.

"Well, you don't have a lot of money, so you can't really complain. You're welcome to leave, but I'm staying. I have enough money for five or six months, depending on how frugal I am with it." I wondered about John's sense of entitlement.

John decided to stay, but I knew he wasn't happy about it. It was like he didn't want to be uncomfortable, or

suffer for any reason. I could put up with it if I had an end goal or light at the end of the tunnel. Besides picking oranges, we also helped out in the bakery. The owners, Althea and Alek, enjoyed our company and spent time teaching us Greek. They would feed us a meal afterwards for payment. More money we didn't have to spend.

The rest of our spare time was spent exploring the island and events in the area, playing guitar, going to Hania for hot showers and shopping, walking everywhere, sightseeing, and hanging out with the locals. That seemed to be all there was to do, unless we took a ferry to Athens. I knew if we went to Athens, we wouldn't return to Crete.

After the first few nights in the building, we all knew it was haunted. There was soft banging on windows, eerie and howling sounds from inside and outside, and footsteps that always disappeared. We would check out the sounds and never find anything. Some nights were worse than others. I wondered if we shouldn't move, but John didn't think it was a problem. We would get used to it. I didn't think so, but my frugal side won out. Money is a powerful motivator.

As we picked oranges one day, I asked, "Is it possible to eat too many oranges?" I now had my eighth orange in my mouth. The keepers kept to themselves, speaking in Greek most of the time.

"No. I don't think so. Your body doesn't store Vitamin C," said Maggie. Jean and John agreed.

I sniffed the overpowering smell of oranges everywhere in the grove. It was ten acres of orange tree after orange tree. I pulled my sweater around me as I climbed the tree to pull off some oranges. Our keepers liked to make sure we worked. They allowed small breaks, plus lunch. I knew I would never do this again in my life, so wanted to savor the moments. I wondered if John drifted in and out of his own world in an effort to escape. I did that sometimes, but knew I had to pay attention. We all had clippers that could be dangerous.

Suddenly an orange peel hit my head. I looked down and John was smiling up at me.

"Just wanted to make sure you were awake."

"How's it going?" I asked, watching him eat an orange.

"You know. Boring, but okay. There's an animal over there I want to see." He pointed at something and raced over to the area. A moment later he returned with a hedgehog, all curled up in his hand. I had my camera and took a picture of them. With John's beard, he actually looked like the hedgehog. He'd been growing it out since we got to Crete. I didn't mind, because I knew this job didn't come easy for him, and I appreciated him sticking it out. Sometimes all of us would sing pop songs and if the Greeks knew them, they would sing along. It was a powerful uniting force, especially through the Beatles songs that everyone knew. It brought all of us closer and formed a camaraderie that wasn't there before.

For me, the haunted house caused tension and restlessness. My sleep was interrupted by howling. I'd explore and come back to bed exhausted. It bothered me more than the rest of the occupants. I would watch John sleeping peacefully, with the moonlight shining across his face and hair. He looked so peaceful that I didn't want to wake him, so I suffered in silence until the morning.

Too much togetherness, sleep deprivation, and feelings of doom were taking their toll on me. No matter how much our psyches meshed, one day I reached my breaking point.

"I don't want to go into Hania and spend money we don't have," I yelled at John.

"I'm not staying here another minute," John said, his voice as loud as mine. "I'm bored and we've been working for over two months now. Let's do something."

"I want to do something, just not this minute. Just go without me."

"Fine. I will. I have no idea when I'm coming back." And with that, he stormed out of the place and slammed the door behind him.

Finally I had peace and quiet, or so I thought. I was boiling water for tea when I heard footsteps outside, then the door opened. The footsteps sounded as if they were right behind me. I turned quickly, but no one was there. I wondered if John had come back and was in one of the rooms. I quickly walked to the front door, but it was closed. I opened it and looked around, then walked around the building. No one was there.

I walked back into the building. As I passed by the living room, a chill went up my spine. I stood in the center of the room and looked up at the chandelier. It looked fine, but as I turned slowly, I saw an apparition of a young man with short dark hair and a beard. He startled me and I opened my mouth to scream. No sound came out of my mouth. I tried again. Nothing. The man floated closer towards me. I stood frozen, unable to do anything. I held my breath and waited. I closed my eyes and then opened them again. He was still there.

"*Don't be frightened. I won't hurt you. I don't even think I can.*" He spoke to me telepathically. I stared at his soft brown eyes and breathed out. He looked harmless enough.

"*What do you want?*" I thought. I initially wanted to run away if I could ever move, but my curiosity got the better of me. I'd always been able to feel ghosts in areas of my parent's house, especially the attic. And once I saw a woman sitting on my bed for a few seconds. But this seemed more intense and desperate. This ghostly apparition chose to show itself to me, so the least I could do was pay attention and help it, even if my skin was crawling and I felt icy cold.

"*Please put flowers on my grave outside the*

window."

"*You mean the kitchen window?*" I shuddered, thinking of the one I always stared at for no particular reason.

"*Yes. The spot you look at sometimes. I know it bothers you... That's because it is my grave.*"

"*Will you go away after this? Will you rest? What happened? If you don't want to tell me, you don't have to.*"

"*Yes, I believe I will rest. What happened to me was an accident and I don't blame anyone. I'm going to start fading soon. So please promise me you'll do what I asked.*"

"*I promise. I'll try to do it today if I can. Even if it's the craziest thing I've ever done, I'll do it. I do keep my word.*"

"*That's why I chose you. And the fact that you sense my presence more than the others. By the way, your water is boiling in the kitchen.*"

"*Thanks.*" I raced to the kitchen to make my tea. When I turned around, the ghost was gone.

Although I looked for flowers, I couldn't find any I liked. I asked Althea if she had any. She said no, but asked if I could help her in the bakery. I agreed, since she and Alek went out of their way for me and John. By the time I got home, I still had no flowers. I thought I would have to go into town, when I heard footsteps and the front door closing.

"Shawna, are you here?" John shouted from the living room.

"I'm in our room," I was searching for my money when John appeared in the doorway with flowers in his hand. He came over and kissed me.

"I'm sorry about our fight."

"Me too. Who are the flowers for?" I felt color drain from my face.

"For you, ninny. Who else would they be for? Why are you so white?" He looked worried.

"I need these for something, actually. Thank you so much." I kissed him lovingly. "They're beautiful." A rainbow of yellow, violet, white, and pink flowers greeted me.

"I don't know the names of them, so don't ask. They're supposed to be local."

"Great." I quickly took them and dashed outside to put them on the spot. John followed me outside.

"Have you gone mad? What are you doing?"

"Putting them in a wonderful spot." I positioned them just right for aesthetics.

"Shawna, what happened when I was gone?" He looked at me as if I was possessed.

"Nothing." I said quickly. John bent down to look at the flowers and then me.

"I know something happened. You don't have to tell me, but we don't keep secrets from each other."

81

"I know. Maybe later. John, why did you buy me flowers? I know you do sometimes, but why today?" I looked at him as we both now stood up.

"It's odd, actually. A woman was selling them, and she practically forced them on me. I knew you'd like them, and she said you needed them. But I didn't know you needed them for this."

"It's good that the flowers are here. Really good. And thank you again for them." We kissed and hugged. But John held me in his arms and then asked me again what happened.

"I'll tell you inside." We walked into the kitchen.

"Well?" John asked. He stood there looking at me.

"I had a visitor while you were gone. That's all."

"What kind?" His eyes narrowed.

"The ghostly kind. Anyway, things should be quieter around here, now that there's flowers on his grave. And don't ask."

"I hope so." But he didn't look convinced, and had a puzzled look on his face. And I'm sure he wondered what his girlfriend had turned into while he'd gone out.

Lesson: Ghosts don't like to be ignored. Just talk to them and find out what they want.

Chapter 13

The next couple of weeks flew by. The hauntings had stopped, and I was sleeping better. We all were. However, we started to notice a change in the local people. It seemed like we were getting shunned, and none of us knew why. The Greeks who had been treating us like gifts from God, were now treating us like "gifts" from Satan. Although we thought it could be our imaginations, my intuition told me something else was going on. It seemed to have started a few days after the flower ceremony. I had no idea why that would be.

"Maybe it's not the flowers. Maybe it's something else." John said as we worked on the same tree.

"I don't know. But something is amiss. I feel it."

"I feel it, too," said Jean. Maggie agreed.

"Does your boyfriend, Georges, know?" I asked Maggie as I watched her pick oranges from a high perch.

"He says he doesn't know, but I think otherwise. He's being coy. And I know when he's lying to me. I don't like it."

"What happened a couple of weeks ago? Asked Jean. She and Kyle spent weekends in Athens.

"Not much," I said quickly. "I put a bouquet of flowers on a spot outside our building. That was it."

"Well, that can't mean anything. These Greeks have

their ways, that's for sure." She stopped to peel and eat an orange.

"Work, work," the keeper yelled out. He couldn't stand us talking together; he probably thought we'd go on strike or something.

"What about Althea and Alek? Have they said anything?" Maggie asked.

"No," said John. "They are acting polite, but not friendly like they used to be. And we've spent a lot of time with them. Maybe they think we're a bad influence on their kids or something. I don't know." He stopped to eat an orange as well. We were all getting short timer's disease, and wanted the picking to be over. It almost was.

"I encourage their son to go to school. I know he skips sometimes," said Maggie.

"I did not know this," I replied.

"We may never find out what's going on," Jean said.

Our keeper was eyeing us cautiously. The eyes and ears of our absentee boss. We all went back to working, but my mind continually thought about the tension in the village.

Another surprise awaited us as we headed to our home. All of our belongings were outside, and Kyle was sitting on the steps, waiting for us.

"The police came and kicked us out. I don't know why. They never gave me a good reason. Just said it was time for us to move on." He was eating a sandwich as he talked. "I think Jean and I will stay on and work at my boss's place. You're all welcome to join us. We could always use an extra set of hands."

"Gee, I think we need to think about that. Right, John?" I looked at John as we picked up our packs. We made sure we had everything. Some of the locals were watching us from a distance.

"I don't know. We're almost done, so I think we'll leave the island. Really no point in staying."

"I plan to stay a little while longer. I'm not done here yet," said Maggie. She probably meant she wasn't done with Georges.

"Well, I'm not happy with what's going on here. I got into a fight with the café owner a few days ago. I don't think that's it, but you never know," said Jean.

"It could be the flowers I set on the grave." I said.

"What flowers on a grave? That shouldn't make any difference," said Kyle, still eating.

"It actually *is* a problem," Maggie said, finally shedding light onto the situation. "Well, there are a couple of things. We've been here awhile, and my dating a Greek is a problem. They think we're a bad influence. And you placed those flowers on a Turk's grave. He died under mysterious circumstances about a year or two ago. No one but the locals know about it. They kept it quiet, and they don't like that we know about it. It's time for us to leave the building and this town. There are other towns just up

85

the road we can stay at."

All of this was news to us.

"Who told you it was the flowers?" I asked.

"Well, Georges did. I didn't want to say anything. Didn't want to hurt anyone's feelings. Plus all the other things I said. It'll just get worse if we stay here." She had rearranged her pack and made sure she had everything.

"I say we take our money and leave," said John. "Although I don't like being run out of town like this."

"Do you want to stay and fight?" I asked. "Because I don't. We don't belong here anymore." The inner demon had spoken again.

"Okay. Let's walk into Hania and then take the ferry to Athens. From there we'll decide where we're going," John said.

"No need to walk," said Maggie. "My friend, the cab driver, can take us there."

"Jean and I are going to walk down the road and hitch a ride to the other farm. Offer still stands," Kyle asked, hoping we would change our minds.

No one took him up on it. We said our goodbyes and watched them walk off.

When the cab arrived, John, Maggie, and I hopped in and braced ourselves for a new adventure.

Lesson: The dead are much easier to understand than the living. That's for sure.

Chapter 14

When we got to Athens, we went to a café for a bite to eat and figure out where we would sleep.

"You know I don't like being homeless. A roof over my head is a necessity. Food is secondary," I said to John as we ate.

"You always worry about it. So far we've been fine." He tried to brush off my concerns.

"Abandoned buildings, squatting, caves, and haystacks. I think I'm done with the rough life. It's not fun, although we make the best of it."

"You have to admit, though, we saved a lot of money by doing that. Or we'd both we home by now."

"True. Still, it's not something I need to repeat." I noticed a young Greek man watching us. After a while, he walked over to us.

"Listen, I couldn't help but overhear you. I have a place on the beach. You can stay there as long as you like. No strings attached. Just return the key to me when you're done. I'll show you where to leave it."

We thanked him, and after eating, followed him to the beach shack. It was a cute wooden structure that had a small bedroom, bathroom, kitchen, and living room. The furnishings were sparse, but adequate. Compared to our last place on Crete, this was a mansion.

After our recent episode with Greek people, we wondered if he would throw us out for unknown reasons, but decided to give him a chance. We needed several days to recharge from toiling in the orchards and upsetting the locals. John had taken it particularly hard for some reason.

"You're just hurt by what happened, right?" I placed my pack on the bed.

"Hurt, annoyed, frustrated. Why didn't they just say they wanted us out, instead of doing it behind our backs while we were at work?" He put his pack down and lay on the bed. "Come here." He opened his arms for me and I snuggled up to him.

"It's a betrayal in a way, right?" I asked him.

"Right. I guess. After all we've done for them, this is how we get repaid."

"It's done. Nothing we can do now. There's a sea between us. Let's figure out where we're going next," I said, resting on his shoulder.

"My friend Jackie will be in Israel in a few days. So I'd like to see her."

"Who told you?" I sat up and looked at him wide eyed.

"My mom. I talked with her when I went into Hania that day we argued." He now sat up as well and looked intently at me.

"You didn't mention it before." I wondered why I was just now hearing about this.

"I forgot. Sorry. I had a lot on my mind."

At this, I pulled my guidebook out of my pack and found the page I wanted.

"I'd like to go to Egypt. The pyramids and Sphinx. I've wanted to see them my whole life. I think we should go there." I showed the page to John.

"And I want to see Israel. Plus we could work on a kibbutz and save money."

"Jackie? Or Israel?" I asked quickly.

"Both. You'd like her. There's nothing going on. She's a friend, like Connor is your friend." I forgot that I had told John about Connor when we were in Crete.

"Maybe we should count our money and then decide. We made quite a bit in Crete and didn't spend much." We pulled out our Greek drachmas and converted them. We had over seven hundred dollars between us, plus my savings. It was close to the middle of March, and we wanted to be in London by June or July. The more places we could work the better. Still, Israel had not been on my itinerary.

"The problem is, we can't cross from Israel into Egypt. We can't get a stamp in our passport, and it can still be difficult. Plus, *now* we have to fly back to Athens, and then to Egypt. Lots more money needed. And we still need to travel to England." Evaluating our money and all the places we still had to see, made me groan. A decision had to be made.

"You're staying with me in London, so that's not a problem. But it will cost us with all the countries and stops we'll be making."

"We could go separate ways and meet up in Athens later on," I said, hoping for a compromise. "You go to Israel and I'll go to Egypt."

"No. That won't work," said John quickly. "We shouldn't be apart like that. I don't like it."

"We'll find each other again. We always do." I really wanted to go to Egypt.

"Why do you say it like that?"

"I don't know. It just came out that way. Why?"

"I think it means something. But I don't know what."

"Focus," I said, getting us on track. "We need to have a plan. Why don't we go to Egypt first, and then see about Israel later?"

"We'd miss Jackie, though. She'd be fun to travel with. And she's getting there next week and staying for two or three weeks. Plus we can save money by working."

"Alright." I gave in, against my better judgment. And it would come back to bite me.

Lesson: Never trust someone else's judgment over your own.

Chapter 15

The flight from Athens to Tel Aviv was uneventful, even though I had an uneasy feeling about the whole thing. And sure enough, our problems started in immigration and customs.

"I don't want a stamp in my passport," I politely said to the Immigration official, a middle-aged Israeli man. He became quite unpleasant and asked for my return ticket to Athens. John and I had not booked them because we weren't sure how long we would be staying. When he heard this, the man called over another officer. This older man with an angular face, dark hair and stormy eyes took me and John into his office, since John also did not want the stamp.

"How much money do you have on you?" he asked us. We told him.

"That will buy your ticket."

"But it won't leave much left over," I explained to him as we sat in chairs in the cramped office.

"Aren't you planning on working in a kibbutz?" he asked abruptly.

"Yes. But it will take time to make arrangements. In the meantime, we're stuck."

John and I exchanged glances. I could feel my blood

pressure rising.

"There is another option. I could deport you both," he said bluntly.

"Where to?" we asked simultaneously.

"You to London, and you to the States," he pointed at each of us. He never cracked a smile.

"Why not Athens? We just came from there," I said.

"Are you from there? Do you have citizenship? I think not," was his brusque reply. "And if we deport you home, you will have to repay your embassies." He snickered as he said this.

John and I stepped outside the office to talk about our situation. We agreed that separating wasn't good, and Athens was out. We'd have to buy the tickets and make do.

Instead we walked back in and I said to the man, "I'd like to be deported to Egypt." John's eyebrows went up as I said this. He hadn't expected this.

"We don't fly there. It's impossible." He glared at me, and I glared back. I loathed this man.

"Alright. I think we'll buy our tickets then," said John trying to keep the peace.

"Let me see your traveler's checks," the officer demanded. I slammed them on his desk, and he looked them over carefully.

"These are in British pounds. We need American dollars. We can exchange them, and that will cost you a bit more." He smiled. We were being had, and we knew it. I felt helpless and angry at myself for getting talked into coming to this horrible place.

We sat there while he left to make the arrangements for our tickets.

"If we needed a return ticket, why didn't the agent tell us?" I asked John.

"I don't know. They didn't have a problem giving us a one-way ticket, though. And do you have to try and piss everyone off? Egypt? Really?" he said, clearly exasperated.

"I figured if they were going to deport us, at least I could go somewhere I really wanted to go."

John continued to look annoyed, but I just shrugged my shoulders at him. It was his fault we were in this mess.

We finally got our tickets and left. Both of us were upset and frustrated with the situation.

"We have like five dollars between us. I hate this place," I told John. "And I wish we hadn't come here." I walked hurriedly through the airport and went outside to get some air. John followed me out, but then stopped in front of me. He put his hands on my shoulders.

"I know you're angry. I know I'm going to get blamed for this."

"You think?" I shouted, "You and your brilliant ideas. This is the worst. I should have said no!" People walking by looked at us. I didn't care. I hoped they would arrest us. At least we'd get meals and a place to sleep.

"Too late now." We walked to a bench and sat down.

We needed to get some fresh air and cool down. We'd almost been deported. My feelings of not belonging and fairness came into play.

I was still complaining when a young Israeli man walked by and heard me.

"Yes. There are a lot of problems here. You have to understand that we are surrounded by enemies and don't trust easily."

"Do we look like we came here to do you harm?" I answered as politely as I could, but it sounded snappy, even to me. I sighed.

"We don't trust easily. I'm sorry." He walked away. By now we had decided the airport would have to be our new home, so we went back inside to search for a place to sleep.

I had allowed John to make a major decision about our travels, and I would never do it again. I couldn't trust him to make the right move.

"Why don't you admit you were wrong about Israel? We shouldn't have come here, and I don't belong here." There was that inner demon I was expecting to hear from. Raising its ugly head to the occasion.

"I'm sorry. I know this is a bad situation, but let's make the best of it. I picked oranges and didn't want to," he said, as if picking oranges was the worst labor he'd ever done.

"And I told you that you could leave. Why is that so hard for you?" We spotted the lounge area and now sat down by ourselves.

"I don't like being away from you, that's all."

"You're kind of needy, aren't you?" I said, now wishing I could take it back. Too late.

"I don't like being alone as much as you do. It's not a crime," he said sullenly.

"Maybe you should live on your own for a while. It might do you some good," I said, glaring at him. I wondered if my temper would ever die down.

"I don't want to. That's all," he said quietly. He looked away, and I wondered what other secrets he might be keeping from me.

"Why are men so helpless? You could rent a flat in London with a few other people, share expenses. That would work."

John looked at me like I had a hole in my head.

"I don't know why we're talking about these things. We have each other now. Doesn't that mean anything?" He wanted to touch me, but he knew better than to poke the bear.

"Of course. I'm more independent than you, that's all. And freedom is important to me. As well as justice and all kinds of things. I don't know why we're talking about this now. I knew you had issues, but now they seem overwhelming."

"Do you want to break up with me? Then do it," he finally said.

"I didn't say that, but one day I might," I fumed at him.

"You're not easy to get along with either," he said, telling me something I already knew.

"Agreed. But I'm not a mean person. I don't do things out of spite. I'm very caring and kind. At least I try to be. I could have ditched you a long time ago, and didn't." Now I wished I'd taken Connor up on his offer, but it was too late. My ethics and integrity wouldn't allow me to.

"I'm going to let that remark slide, because I know you're still furious. Let's see if we can find something to eat. We're both unhappy about being here, but I'll try to make it up to you. I really will. I'm sorry."

He looked so sad that I let him kiss me; then we headed toward the cafes and shops. We were still talking about our money woes when a female airport worker came up to us.

"I'm sorry," she said in a crisp English accent, "but I couldn't help overhearing you. I could help you out some, not with money, but food vouchers at the airport."

We looked down at this petite woman, unable to believe our good luck. She had short dark hair, a small nose, and a wide mouth. Her name was Mable, and as far as I was concerned, she was an angel.

Mable and John reminisced about England while I listened. She'd been in Israel for several years, and this was her home now. We exchanged travel stories, and then she gave us vouchers worth ten dollars apiece. She offered to get us more if we needed them. She also gave us info on the kibbutz situation and showed us around the terminal. We would need to get a physical, and if we passed, meet with a coordinator to pick out the one we wanted.

We thanked her and got something to eat.

"See. It's not so bad." John tried to get me to smile, but I wouldn't.

"I'm not happy yet. This place has left me cold. Europe warm. Big contrast to what we've experienced elsewhere. You'd think I was German." I said, munching on a sandwich.

"You look like you could be. No offense. I know you're not."

"Maybe I should put on a Nazi uniform. Stir things up. It can't get any worse."

"Don't even think about that. You'll get us both killed." John looked around to make sure no one heard us.

"So where is this Jackie friend of yours?"

"I should call and find out."

After we finished eating we found a phone and John placed a call to his parents. He spoke to them for several minutes, then handed the phone to me so I could talk to them. I hung up a few minutes later and looked expectantly at John.

"Okay. So where is she?"

"Don't get mad, okay? She changed her mind and

went to Egypt instead." John covered his face in anticipation of my reaction.

"No way. She's in Egypt and we're here? John, I hate her. I mean, I really, really hate her." I glared at him. "One of these days you're really going to get hurt. Seriously."

"I know. I feel the same way. I would have made a different decision if I had known."

"Your judgment sucks. You know that, right?"

"I'm not perfect. Are you happy now?"

"No. But it's a start." We made our way back to our airport bedroom for the next couple of days.

Lesson: Some places are better for you than others. Live in or visit the ones that contribute to your wellbeing, and avoid the ones that don't.

Chapter 16

Guns were everywhere in Israel. I often wondered when I might get shot at. Women in military garb carried big machine guns, as well. I wanted one of them.

"I could carry one of the guns and have a lot of fun here," I joked to John as we hitched to our kibbutz.

"They'll never let you have one, thank goodness. You can be a real spitfire at times, you know that? But I also like that about you. You don't back down like a lot of women do."

"Yes, I know. A girl can dream, can't she?" I asked, eyeing several men with guns as they hopped into vehicles after hitchhiking.

"As long as the military personnel are out here hitchhiking, we're never going to get a lift. We'll have to wait until they clear out." He sat at the side of the road under some shade. I joined him.

I started thinking about the physical we had just completed, so we could work on the kibbutz. It seemed odd that young people would need one. I didn't need one to pick oranges in Greece.

"That physical for the kibbutz was strange," I said to John. "That perverted old doctor didn't even put a gown on me when he examined my chest. What a dirty old man!"

Another injustice added to the many I kept in my head. Israel had to be the worst place in the whole world. It *had* to be.

"Yeah. That's too bad. At least you passed," he said, sipping water. He offered some to me.

"They would have passed a person who was almost dead. It's a joke. They have more rules and regulations than a Communist country. You know that?" I said, gulping the water. "Why is Israel so hot? I feel like I'm back in Florida." Another strike.

"It seems that way, yes. Can you let it go now? I think you like being aggravated," he said calmly.

"I like fairness and justice. Especially fairness. That's not much to ask." I glared briefly at John to make my point.

"You might as well kiss fairness goodbye. Not going to happen, and you and I have to live with it."

"Fine. But I don't have to like it." Finally, the soldiers had all gotten rides, so we stuck out our thumbs, and got a lift to the kibbutz.

Our kibbutz was small compared to others we could have chosen from, but we didn't want to be near the border conflicts. Good for us, since I would have made an escape into the Arab countries. For better or worse.

We toured the farm on our own. We held our noses as we passed the dairy area where cows grazed. It reeked of manure, and we watched where we stepped in the grass.

We saw many more cows in the barns as well, as we strode quickly out of the stench. We passed greenhouses and large garden areas. We stopped to watch the children in the playground area. The children were segregated from their parents and had their own sleeping quarters. The families only visited each other at meals and evenings, plus weekends.

"It must be strange, not having your children live with you all the time," I said to John.

"Yes. Gives you freedom, though. What do you think? Do you think we'll have one of them one day?" He squeezed my hand, and I looked up at him. He seemed serious.

"Maybe. We have to get married first. And have a stable income." I thought if my recurring dream came true, I would end up raising a child on my own. The worst thing for my independent nature. I vowed never to have a child with him until I was absolutely sure he wouldn't die. No skydiving for him. John agreed, especially with the financial part. He liked having money, but didn't like working for it. I secretly wondered if he had any ambition.

We made our way to the visitor's lounge, where we were given our work assignments and living arrangements. Since we weren't married, I knew we would be staying in separate quarters. John was not happy about this. Deportation, fine. Sleeping in airports, fine. No money, fine. Can't sleep with me, *not* fine. I laughed.

"It's not funny," he said, as we made our way to our dorms.

"It's a hostel all over again. At least it's not an abandoned building."

"Well, I don't like it. I'm going to talk to them." John seemed visibly upset, and I couldn't understand why. I watched him walk off to the administration building.

I entered my dorm room to find three beds. Two were already occupied, so I put my bag down on the empty one and looked around. We had our own restroom. The walls were blue and we had sparse furnishings. My roommates had decorated the place with their own art and photos. It was homey. About ten minutes later, John showed up.

"They don't have a house for us, but they put us on the waiting list." John looked around at my new home. "It's nice. Better than mine."

"How do you feel about your work assignment? Milking cows and such?" I asked. I already knew we wouldn't be staying here for long.

"It's not great. But I'll be fine. Yours isn't good either. Picking roses?"

"I know. We just picked oranges. More labor. I can do it. Not sure how long, though." I looked at his dejected face as he sat in one of the chairs.

"Do you think I can sleep with you tonight?" He eyed my single bed.

"It's small. I don't know. My roommates might not

like it. It's really up to them." I felt for sure they would not agree to this.

About ten minutes later my roommates arrived. Sheri had reddish brown hair, a small nose, and green eyes. Her face was scattered with freckles. She had a friendly smile. Arlene had curly brown hair with brown eyes. Both were adorable. I felt lucky.

"Not a problem," said Sheri, much to my surprise when John asked them. Adele also agreed. Both were from England and took an immediate liking to him. They talked about England for some time, and then John kissed me before leaving.

"Are you sure you're okay with it?" I asked both of them when he was gone. "Because he has a dorm."

"No. It's lovely. He likes being with you. And we don't mind, really." She brushed back her reddish brown hair.

"What is your job?" asked Arlene. She had a slightly rounder face than Sheri and was very cute.

I told her my job and she said she worked in the greenhouse as well. Sheri worked with the children. A cushy job, if you can get it. The bell rang for dinner and we headed to the dining room. The large room housed lots of long tables and chairs, and the food was served cafeteria-style. I loaded up my plate and sat with John. Other foreigners sat with us. I noticed the Israelis sitting and talking Hebrew amongst themselves. Then the children showed up after dinner to be with their parents. The kibbutz life would take some getting used to.

Several days later, John was complaining of his work assignment, as usual. I wasn't happy with the way I was being treated in the greenhouse either. The Israelis kept to themselves and watched over us carefully. They were not very friendly, and it made me appreciate how Yanni and his workers treated us.

"When should we leave?" he asked me after dinner. We had gone outside and found a quiet spot to talk in private.

"We got paid for two weeks, so I'd like to stay that long. Or close to it. I don't feel right taking money I haven't earned." We had cashed in our tokens after receiving them on the first day.

"Two weeks. But that's it. I do like the cows, though. They're so gentle and their beautiful, large eyes are captivating. Still, we never planned on staying a long time."

"Right. I know. We gave it a try. I like to experience new things, so this was good. I'll miss my roommates, though."

"Yes. They've been brilliant."

And one night after everyone slept, John and I snuck out, as if escaping from a prison. I kept looking back to see if anyone was following us. They weren't.

We found a field a few miles down the road and put our sleeping bags down. As we lay in each other's arms, looking at the stars, I pointed to one and said, "I come from that star, far, far away." I knew what I said had some truth to it.

"But that's the one I come from," said John, gazing at it.

"Then it's a miracle we found each other."

"I think you and I always know how to do this. It's easy for us." He kissed me gently, and we cuddled for some time.

Lesson: Remember where you come from. And if you don't know, keep asking.

Chapter 17

We stayed in Jerusalem for ten days and explored the sights before heading back to England. We both enjoyed Jerusalem and the Dead Sea, plus Bethlehem.

As usual, Israel kicked us out the door for good measure. We both got strip searched at the airport. After that ordeal, I said to John, "I despise Israel and I am never coming back here, even if God herself shows up." I picked up my pack and headed for the plane. "The way they treat foreigners, no one should come here."

"The good news is you don't have to. I didn't enjoy it either." He put on his pack. The way the Israelis had treated us didn't seem to offend him like it did me.

Money became more precious, as it slowly dwindled through my fingers. We had enough to return home, stop and see several cities we missed, and that was it. My money had lasted ten months, and that included paying for John's part as well. In spite of everything, it had been worth it. We planned to hitchhike most of the time and take trains or buses if the weather got bad. And soon, I'd meet his parents.

As I walked up the steps of their Tudor home, I felt a bit anxious about meeting them, but to my relief, they quickly hugged and welcomed me in. John's dad, Claude, looked like an older version of his son with shorter hair. About half of it was grey, which made him look very distinguished. His mother had blond hair and blue eyes. Tall and thin, she looked almost elegant. We spent the next three weeks getting acquainted before I headed home.

John wanted to spend time with me, but I talked him into going to work. We'd already spent plenty of time together. He worked building boats with his dad, since it paid more money. I knew it wasn't his first choice, but then I didn't know if John even had a first choice. If he did, he kept it close to his chest. He'd given up his dream of playing in a band some time ago.

During the three weeks I spent with John's family, I met his friends, including Jackie. She turned out to be as nice as John said, but she was a flake. That explained the mix-up in Israel. Roger was John's best friend, and he taught guitar and showed John more songs. They both liked punk and rock music, plus all the great classics. John's favorite guitarist was Jimmy Page, who he always raved about.

One weekend we headed for Petticoat Lane, so I could get some souvenirs and clothes. The sheer size of it told me it could take all day to see. The hordes of people crowded around the various vendors selling everything you could imagine. John and I pushed our way through, ignoring the vendors who tried to bargain with us. The smell of oranges, tomatoes, cinnamon, and floral flavors all mixed together in my nostrils. Visual and olfactory stimuli bombarded me from every corner, it seemed. It could get you dizzy if you weren't used to it.

"It's chaotic," I said when we finally found a less crowded spot away from the masses.

"It's always like this," John said. "And this is early yet. The afternoon will be worse." We stood looking at the sights around us. "At least you found some tee-shirts."

We headed for a woman sitting in the shade. As I got closer, I saw she was a palm reader named Madame Helen.

"I'm going to have a reading," I said as I got closer. "Do you want one?" I looked at him.

"I don't know. I might. I want to hear what she says to you first."

I sat opposite the middle-aged woman with shoulder-length dark hair and intense blue eyes. She watched me carefully and I didn't take my eyes off of her. I placed my palms out for her to read.

"First of all, you could be doing my job. You're very intuitive. And yet, you also have a healer's hands. What do you do now?" I told her. "You'll have at least four careers or more in this lifetime. You can do anything you put your mind to, but you already know that." She continued to study my palms. Then she looked at John for several seconds. John got the hint and went to get something to drink. "I'll see you soon," he said as he went off into the crowd. I watched him leave.

"I don't normally do that, but you have an interesting hand. Very Atlantis." I nodded. I'd always felt an affinity for it. "You will have more than one marriage. And at least one or two romantic attachments. A long, healthy life. You come from a Star. I'm not sure of the name. It's unusual. And you feel you don't belong here because of that. You do belong, though, because you came here to serve and spread light. You will help lots of people in your lifetime. You could be a teacher as well. Remember that you have choices. So do others. Sometimes their bad choices affect others. It's a conundrum, that's for sure. You don't like people telling you what to do, and you value freedom and independence more than anything."

"Will I marry the man you saw me with?" I asked before our time is up.

"Yes, but you do have two choices on that one. You two have a soul connection and the angels smiled when you met. Time is precious and short here on earth. Enjoy it." I thanked her and paid her. Then she said, "Remember your dreams. They speak to you." I had been blown away by her reading. She confirmed everything that I thought about myself. Especially the Star and Atlantis part.

John returned and sat down. I was going to leave, but John asked me to stay and Madame Helen gave her okay. She looked at John's hands carefully. She finally said, "Maybe it's best I don't read for you today."

"Why? Is something wrong?" John's eyebrows creased

and all color left his face.

"I'll read a bit for you. She hesitated, then went on. "First, your fate and life lines are overlapping. That's not the best position. It means you have to be extra careful with the decisions you make in your life. Which means you can't afford to make a mistake or take risks like other people. You're sensitive and others take advantage of you, but when you know about it you quickly retaliate. You do that overtly or softly. You like to avoid or run away from problems rather than face them head on. Confrontation is not your thing. As for careers, you could be a good musician if you work hard at it. Your destiny is in your hands, but fate and karma will not be messed with. There is no getting around them. No one can save you and that's a good thing. You get to save yourself. The question is, will you? You need to apply yourself for careers and find something that works for you. That way you can do the great things you came here to do.

"I don't see you having any children," she continued, "but of course that can change. And one marriage."

"Great. Thanks so much. You didn't say if I had a long lifeline." John now stood up.

She hesitated before answering. I held my breath. "It's totally up to you."

John nodded and we left. He knew she wouldn't say anything more.

"I don't know about all that. Mine wasn't that great."

We walked through the throngs of people.

"There was nothing really bad about it. You have to make good choices, which to me means doing the right thing. That's all you have to do. How hard is that?" I asked him.

As it turned out, it would be very hard for John to do the right thing.

Lesson: You reap what you sow.

Chapter 18

John brooded for days about his reading. Now I wished he hadn't had one. While I packed my belongings in his bedroom, I tried to cheer him up.

"Well, Madame Helen said I was going to marry a tall, dark, handsome lawyer and have two children. We'll live in an elegant mansion in New York. He's Jewish and he promises me I'll never have to go to Israel." John and I started laughing.

"If you ever go back to Israel…" John paused. "No. I can't even think about it. Thanks for trying to cheer me up." He kissed me gently. I knew he was trying to get romantic, but I needed to finish packing my bag.

"Right. So, I'm leaving tomorrow." I pushed him away mildly. "Hard to believe I'm finally going home."

"You have a Cockney accent now. Didn't take long for you to pick that up."

"I know, right? How fun. There, I'm finally done." I had a backpack and a small tote to take on the plane.

"What do you want to do on our last night?" I asked John. I lay down on the bed beside him, and he put his arm around me and asked me to stay.

"I can't. I wish I could, but I have to go home. I hardly have any money and I need to earn some. And I miss my family and friends."

"I want to go with you. You know that, right?"

"I'd like you to fly across the Atlantic. Soon we'll be together again."

"Is that a promise?" He looked intently into my eyes.

"How come I'm making all the promises? What are you promising me?"

John wouldn't answer. He looked away and then said, "You'll see. I have lots of things up my sleeve."

"You have a hairy arm up your sleeve," I said, as I tried to roll up his left sleeve. Then he started tickling me, and the game was on. We finally realized how much noise we were making when we heard his mom on the stairs, asking us to please be quiet.

That night we went to a restaurant, then John ushered me over to the famous Hyde Park. I had wonderful memories of it, when Lyn and I were here. I looked around in awe at the lovely trails, trees, and well-kept flower gardens everywhere; an oasis in the mania of London. We sat near the Serpentine Pond to contemplate the future of our relationship.

John put his arm around me and kissed me. "I love you, Shawna. More than anything. Even after our trip, I hope you still love me."

"I love you, too." I leaned over and put my head on his chest. "Remember when we met in Paris?"

"I'll never forget it. Not ever." I was lost in my

memories of Paris when John showed a closed fist near me. I glanced at it, and then he opened it up to reveal a beautiful ring. I gasped.

"Will you marry me?" he asked sweetly. I looked at him in complete shock. As close as we had gotten, I'd never expected this. Normally, I would have thought it was too soon, but I felt I'd known John for years, rather than months. I couldn't be certain if it had to do with the travel, or the fact that we seemed to know each other so well, almost from the start.

"Yes! Of course I will marry you!" I threw my arms around him and kissed him. "I love this ring." It was flower-shaped with sapphires and diamonds. "I had no idea." I said loudly. "How did you get the money?"

"I'm not going to tell you that." I thought of John's guitar and realized he hadn't serenaded me with it recently. Plus he made good money with his dad.

"You sold your guitar, didn't you?" I asked.

He looked away. "Yes. The ring was more important. I hope you like it."

"Very much. It is so me. It's perfect." I said quietly. "Now I'll have to say no to that rich lawyer when he shows up." I smiled. He grinned, then kissed me passionately.

I looked at the ring again, then up at the full moon, showing her true glory from behind the clouds. The woman in the moon looked at me, and I was sure I saw her wink. I laughed and said, "Didn't Pink Floyd have a song called 'Shine on You Crazy Diamond'?"

"Yes, and now this diamond is shining. How fortuitous," he said, eying the ring.

I was about to correct him and use the word fate instead, but decided against it. There had been too much of that in my life already.

Lesson: The choices you make affect your destiny. Be careful what you choose.

Chapter 19

The plane landed in Miami and I did not want to get off. I wanted to stay on the plane and fly back to London. America felt foreign to me. I didn't belong here anymore. The stewardess came over and politely told me I needed to leave. Sighing, I grabbed my backpack and left the safety of the plane for a familiar city I didn't want to be in. I had culture shock in my own country. Who knew? I took a taxi to my parents' home, knowing my arrival would be a big surprise. I hadn't told anyone of my return plans.

I entered the house and walked in slowly. When I walked into the kitchen, my mother looked at me and screamed. I said quickly, "It's only me. I'm home." My mother's scared expression turned to relief as she recognized her wayward daughter who'd finally come home. Her eyes lighting up, she came over and we hugged and kissed. I'd really missed her and the rest of my family, even though I felt like my new home was back in London.

"It's so good to see you again. I missed you. But please don't scare me like that. You could have given me a heart attack." She examined me carefully. "Shawna, you look like a refugee. What's happened to you?" As soon as she said this, I laughed.

"I've been slumming for a long time. I'm thin and my

hair needs cutting."

"That's for sure. And you sound like you have marbles in your mouth! I can barely understand you with that English accent. I hope you know how much we missed you and worried about you. Especially when you told us about Israel."

I smiled and nodded, then explained that English accents seemed easy for me to pick up, and being around John made it a whole lot easier.

She nodded and smiled, then offered to make me something to eat.

"Thanks, but I'm not hungry. I need to get cleaned up and unpack."

As I sauntered upstairs, I realized I'd always been a refugee in this family, but today I received confirmation. I unpacked and found a card John had stuck in my pack. I opened it. It read,

To my Lovely Sunshine, I wait with bated breath for your return. I want and love you so much. Return in one piece to the man who loves your precious heart.

You're in my heart, always and forever. Love, John.

P.S. Please don't forget about me.

I hugged the card to my heart and kissed it. I missed him already. Such a romantic.

I went back downstairs. My mom hadn't noticed my engagement ring. I didn't say a word about it, and instead told her stories of all the places and people we'd met, especially Lyn.

"Did you see the Pope when you and John were in Rome?"

"Yes, we did. Rome is an interesting place, for sure. But I think Yugoslavia has to have the nicest people in all of Europe. After picking us up hitchhiking, they would offer us beds in their homes and feed us. They were the best. And Dubrovnik has to be one of the best coastal cities. But there are so many to choose from." While I talked I waved my hands a lot.

"Is that an engagement ring?" she shrieked. She had finally noticed it.

"Yes," I said, unable to hide my smile.

"I wasn't expecting it! Were you?"

"No. It was a surprise to me as well." I held it out for her to see.

"It's very nice. We haven't even met him, but hopefully we will soon." She sat back down and drank her coffee. She seemed to have a secret she wouldn't share, and didn't say anything more.

"He won't be here for some time. And I need to go back to work."

"And then what?" Before I had a chance to answer, Aunt Emma showed up.

"You're home. What a wonderful surprise! And you got engaged?" she gasped when she saw my ring. She was much more astute than my mother. "Tell us about him."

I told them everything I knew about John, and showed them photos.

"He sounds almost perfect," said Aunt Emma as she sipped coffee.

"Almost?" I asked.

"You have to admit his finances are not the best, but love is blind, as they say." She glanced at me as if peering into my soul.

"I hope you have both eyes open with this guy, but it's your life," said my mom. She had a detached manner with me. Still, I knew she wanted the best for me and loved me, and that's all I could ask for from this fake family of mine.

"I think so. We have such a great connection and the way we met was no coincidence." I told them how it had happened.

"You were destined to meet a long time ago. It can only mean you're meant to do great things together. It's up to you two to discover what they are." Aunt Emma had a glazed look in her eyes as she spoke, and chills climbed up and down my spine.

"And I suppose your mother has told you the good news?" She glanced over at my mom, who shook her head.

"I was planning on saying something tonight, but I guess I can tell you the surprise." She hesitated and I waited. My parents were not into surprises, so this had to be good.

"Your father and I, plus Gina and cousin Dean, will be

flying to Europe in a few weeks. We were going to go over and surprise you there, but since you came home unannounced, it's kind of spoiled now." She sighed.

"I'm sorry. I didn't know. The good news is you can probably stay with John's parents while you're in London. That is one of the places you're going, right?" I sipped my coffee.

"Yes. I hope you can make the arrangements for that. Gina and Dean are taking a three-week vacation and planning on tours everywhere, with a longer stop in London."

"See what you've done?" said Aunt Emma with a smile. "Everyone wants to travel now. You've started a trend." She winked at me. "The old fogies want to travel after all."

"Give me the dates so the next time I talk to John we can make arrangements." As if he'd heard me, the phone rang and it was John.

"I called to make sure you made it home alright. I miss you so much already."

"I miss you too. Thanks for the card. It was lovely."

"Thanks for the love letter you left me. I'll cherish it always. When are you coming back?"

"I don't know. But in a few months I should have enough money."

"You have a visa. You can work here, too, you know."

"True. I'd thought of that, but I wanted to use my

ticket. I paid a lot for it. And I wanted to visit everyone here and tell them about my adventure."

John assured me that my parents were welcome, but just to be certain, he would ask his family and get back to me. After much love and kisses, we hung up.

I let my mom know the situation, then I asked Aunt Emma when we could talk to each other privately. I needed her intuition and psychic ability more than ever.

Lesson: Family is your soul connections, and not just blood relatives.

Chapter 20

With my parents in Europe, I had the house to myself. Gina had moved into a nice apartment in Miami and was thriving there. She and Dean, a cousin on my dad's side, had taken off to Europe on the same flight. They gave me their itineraries in case something happened.

I had started back at my old agency job, working all over Miami. Now, working felt like a vacation. Who knew? John and I continued to make constant phone calls and write letters. He wanted to fly here, but I discouraged him. He needed to save money, and he couldn't work in the States.

"Why can't I fly to Miami? Don't you want to see me?" he said, almost whining.

"John, you can't work here. I don't know anyone who would hire you. Anyway, I'll be there soon enough. You can live without me for a few months. Good grief, after all our time together, don't you want a break?" I certainly needed one, but I didn't tell him that. I wondered how we didn't kill each other with all the togetherness day in and day out.

"Not really. I mean, I don't like it here."

"You don't like living with your parents, or you don't like your job?"

"Both, actually. My parents are all right. They just

don't understand me."

"Welcome to my world. My dad is better at it than my mom, at least, but my sister is clueless."

"I don't act this way around every female I'm involved with. I know you think that's not true."

"You read my mind."

"You're the first person who gets me. And we have this amazing chemistry together."

"Yes, we do." I remembered how romantic John could be. His sweet kisses and touches sent hot blood flowing throughout my body. My heart raced a little just thinking about him.

"Okay. I'll do what you ask, but I don't like it." I was brought back to reality by John's voice.

"Fine. Besides, you have to meet my parents. Or did you forget? And my sister and Cousin Dean, too."

"They might not like me. Then what? It's easier for the female than the male in these situations."

"I agree. Just be your kind self. The one everyone seems to like." And with that, we finally ended our conversation. I needed to see Aunt Emma so she could give me insight. As soon as John and I hung up, I called my aunt and invited myself over.

An hour later, we were sitting in her den. It had lots of bookshelves, but I preferred to look at the pictures of East Indian gurus and saints, especially the one with Babaji the Immortal. He always looked so young and blissful, even though he was supposed to be hundreds of years old. There were also pictures of Jesus, Buddha, Shiva, Quan Yin, and many more. A cultural mesh of several belief systems blending nicely together. No strife allowed at Aunt Emma's.

"Cards or tea?" she asked me.

"Cards for a change." I replied still looking at the photos on the wall.

"Alright. Shuffle them and cut them into three piles. And then pick one." I did as I was told. She turned the cards over from the middle deck and started reading.

"More travel for you, but this trip will not be so long. Maybe a couple months. Are you buying a vehicle?"

"I don't think so. Trains are better."

"If you do, make sure it's in good shape. And plan your trip carefully. Make sure you have the correct visas and you know where you're going. You two will have some disagreements on this one."

"Yeah. The last one was stress free," I said sarcastically. She smiled knowingly.

"You were getting to know each other. You both can be stubborn. John sometimes doesn't think before he acts. The two of you have to learn not to take external things out on each other."

"True."

"You don't trust his judgment and he knows that. He has hunches as well. If you can accept the fact that he may never support you in the lifestyle you want, then things can be fine. But you don't always like being the breadwinner. You work hard for your money, and you expect your partner to do the same. So the question is, do you stay with someone knowing all of this?" She paused, then added, "He loves you deeply. More than you love him. And that's a good thing in a relationship. Can you be happy? Yes. No question. He can always work, but he's particular about the jobs he has. If he doesn't like it, he won't stay. And that bothers you. You would stay until you found something else. He won't do that." Aunt Emma held my gaze. "You have a choice to make. He'll always be there for you, even when it seems like he's not. The two of you often meet in dream time, and both of you feel what the other is going through. That is a blessing and a curse. You both trust and understand each other. And deep down you are friends. So lots to think about."

"We've been together in past lives, correct?"

"Yes. Many times. You are soul mates. And you're opening up more to the unknown and questioning where you're going and why. That's good. And that's why you feel you know each other already."

"If we've done this so many times, maybe I should find someone else to play with this time?" I question why I'm picking the same person.

"It's all about contracts and what you both set out to do. And you will find other playmates. John may not be your only mate."

"Does that mean my dream will come true?"

"It's not a sure thing. It depends on John. Like all of us in life, he has choices to make. And each one causes a domino effect that creates karma and fate. One thing is for sure, though: do not have children with this man."

"Why?" I asked quickly. I felt she could read my mind.

"It wouldn't be the best choice. I don't know if you can live with that decision or not. How important are children to both of you?" She peered into my eyes.

"We've talked about it from time to time. I thought I was pregnant once when we were traveling, and neither of us liked the idea. Well, the whole situation would have been a disaster. Thank goodness I wasn't. That's all I can say." I breathed a sigh of relief, remembering how tense we both had been since neither of us had the money. John told me how careful he was about contraception since his financial situation was usually grim.

"Have you ever thought of living in Paris?"

"We have talked about that from time to time."

"That might happen, but it's quite a ways down the road. You might want to get readings from other oracles. Just for clarification and insight. And listen to your dreams." She patted my hand.

I thanked her and gave her my gift. A crystal ball that she had always wanted. Her eyes widened and her face lit up. I knew it would be perfect for her.

When I arrived home, I had a letter from Connor waiting for me in the mailbox.

Lesson: Knowing your future doesn't always help you make the right decision.

Chapter 21

Connor's letter told me all about his travels. I realized that he had feelings for me and wondered if I should tell him about John. But I didn't want to give up Connor. For some reason, I couldn't—or wouldn't--but I didn't know why. I think deep down I was afraid that things weren't going to work out with John. As much as I loved him, I didn't think his work ethic was very good, and that concerned me. Everything else about him was great, yet I had almost convinced myself to break up with him by the time my parents came home.

They all raved about John and his family. Everyone had a great time—even my sister. In fact, she returned feeling like she could live in London. All people have to do is visit another country to open their eyes to new possibilities. However, the London honeymoon did not last long. Before I knew it, my sister floated to Miami heaven again, and I dived down to my usual Miami hell.

Soon I had enough money to go back to London. I wasn't too concerned about jobs and felt I could find one. I missed John and wanted to be with him.

"It seems you just got here," said Mom when I told my parents my plan after dinner one evening.

"I know. But it's time to go." We sat in the living room

to talk. I'd been working for several months now.

"I know we haven't talked about it, but what about school?" asked Dad, concerned his daughter was forsaking her education for London.

"I plan to go one day. Probably something medical."

"That's news. What changed your mind?" He eyed me intently, looking for the truth.

"If you must know, a palm reader in London changed my mind." I held my breath, and waited for the laughter. But there was none.

"I can see that," Dad said curiously. "You always liked helping others. Makes sense. What else did she say?"

I told both my parents about the reading.

"Interesting. I never knew they could be so accurate." He seemed amused at the whole thing.

"Well, Emma has psychic abilities," said mom. "She's pretty good, if I remember. Used to read for kids in school, until they made fun of her. Of course after everything she said came true, they stopped that quickly. I should get a reading from her. I haven't had one in a long, long time."

"Has Gina ever had one?" I asked Mom.

"I don't think so. Or if she did, she didn't like it and that was that."

"That sounds like Gina. My critical sister never likes it when anything negative is aimed at her."

"So what happens in London? That's not where you're getting married, right? We want you married here, and as your father I won't take no for an answer."

His seriousness took me by surprise. "Fine. If I get married it'll be here."

"What do you mean, if?" Mom leaned closer to me.

"Well, I'm not sure about anything. All I know is that this long distance relationship is not working for me anymore." I didn't tell them about Connor, and wondered why I had such deep regard for him.

Of course, Connor melted into the back of my brain when I saw John at the airport. He twirled me around and gave me some flowers. It seemed we kissed and hugged forever. He made me happy.

"It feels like a homecoming. I love London," I said to him as he finally put me down.

"Yeah. Your face lights up when you say the name. Here I thought it was just me." He gave me a wry smile.

"And you, too. I'm planning on working here, so then what?" I was already thinking about my future.

"We'll figure something out." John strapped on my backpack. "You could bring a suitcase, you know, but I don't mind. I'm just glad you're here."

"I'm carrying a small tote. Besides, I like traveling light. It's the way to go. So you saw my parents? I know you said they seemed like good people. Anything else?"

"Well, your dad scares me. He gave me a hard time about school when we talked in private. He thinks I should get a better education and make something of myself. He's worse than my father. How do you put up with him?" He looked at me closely as we walked to the tube station.

"He's really wonderful. Very supportive of his daughters. He only wants the best for us and doesn't want to see us hurt." I looked away for a minute. "Oh, and I just wanted to let you know, I'm still in touch with Sam, my ex-fiancé. He sends his regards. He's upset that I'm engaged because he still loves me." I glanced at John, then quickly looked away again. I wanted to tell him the truth, but didn't want to hurt him.

"He still loves you. How do you know that?" He stopped me to peer at me intently.

"Because he told me. We still talk either by phone or letter. But I'm done with him and he knows that. Once I'm done, I'm done. I told you that a long time ago. Plus, there's Connor." Again, I averted my eyes.

"Who's Connor again?" He crinkled his forehead, trying to remember.

"Canary Islands Connor, remember?" I stared wide-eyed at John.

"Yeah, I remember that. You sure keep in touch with male exes and acquaintances."

"You do, too. At least Jackie. I don't know about Natalie."

"Don't mention her name," he looked around quickly.

"If she still disturbs you, then maybe you should talk with her." I noticed a frightened look in his eyes.

"No. I'm done. And so are we with this conversation." John became quiet. Clearly, Natalie still hit a nerve, like she still had some kind of control over him. He'd told me the story, but why did it still bother him? I figured I might never know, but I didn't want her invading our relationship.

We were quiet most of the way to John's home. But when we got off the tube and started walking, he took me in his arms and kissed me.

"I'm sorry. I just don't want to talk about it. It's in the past."

"You realize she will be a force in our relationship if you don't correctly end this relationship. You can't keep doing this."

"I know. I may have to see her, even though I don't want to."

Obviously something was up with them.

"It's the smart thing to do. You know that. I encourage you to see her."

"And what about Connor? I see the way your face lights up when you talk about him."

"Well, he was a nice guy and we had chemistry. Maybe not as intense as ours, but it was there. You know we always want something we can't have." But even as I said the words, I wondered if I could have Connor.

"That's true. What do you want this Christmas?"

"It's still two or three months away. And I have no

idea. Surprise me like you did last time. Good grief, we spent our first Christmas together in Greece. It seems so long ago."

"How do you feel about traveling again?" John asked as we walked to his parents' place. "This time in a van..." I quickly interrupted him.

"I just got here, so ask me in a month or so. Why?"

"My friend Roger knows a couple in Amsterdam who want to sell a van. Not right now. When they're done traveling. A few months, perhaps."

We climbed up the stairs to his room, where I began to unpack. He pulled out a map and plotted an escape route.

"How's work going?" I asked as I put my clothes away.

"It's going. You know, boring at times. But I stick it out because of you, so you're a good influence, I guess." He smiled at me, then turned back to the map.

"You're such a dreamer." I turned to look as I hung up my clothes.

"Yes. And so are you," he said, smiling. I decided to leave well enough alone.

I found an agency job easily and started doing computer work. For a break, I did secretarial work once in a while. I enjoyed the variety. John kept working with his dad and moaning about how hard it was. I didn't want to hear about it. My belief was hard work never hurt anyone.

I finally convinced John to talk to Natalie. He wasn't

happy about it, but he was relieved when he returned after their conversation. They had both needed closure, and she had met someone else. Perhaps now, she would be gone forever from our relationship.

Christmas came around, and I bought John a guitar. He lovingly fingered it and smiled at me after opening it.

"This is the best gift I've ever received. Thank you! It's beautiful. Just want I wanted." He kissed me. "Now open your gift."

I opened the jewelry box and stared at the heart-shaped diamond necklace and earrings he bought. "They're gorgeous. You have such good taste in jewelry. I love it, and I love you." I kissed him back. "We overdid it this year."

"We didn't do so good last year. Neither of us wanted to spend the money, which was understandable. But this year we have no excuse. We've saved a lot."

"We've done well since our travels. It helps with both of us making good money."

My doubts about our future had dissipated when I arrived in London. Life clicked along, and we were happy. My intuition told me to be wary, but I ignored it. Shame on me.

Lesson: Once you end a relationship in a positive way, there's only clear sailing.

Chapter 22

I don't know why, but the idea of a second European trip bothered me. I had never liked repeating myself, and that included work, travel, and activities. This trip felt just like that. I tried to be enthusiastic about our travel plans, but my heart just wasn't in it. By the time we got to Amsterdam and looked at the van, I wanted to leave. I wanted to say something, but I knew that John had big plans. I had been worrying about his big plans since Israel. I thought of Aunt Emma's warning.

We looked over the van, and the nice Australian couple assured us that it would run fine. We took it for a drive and it seemed okay.

"Look at this way, Shawna. We can sleep in it. No more camping out. Your home is right here." He patted the top of the van. As usual, my frugal side won out.

"Something doesn't seem right, but I can't put my finger on it."

"Not to worry. What can go wrong?" The dreamer had spoken.

The trip would include Amsterdam, Belgium, France, and Africa, by way of Spain. It was a trip I had already taken. I knew John missed some of the places, so I told myself I would be alright with it. I would be able to visit some cities I'd missed the first time.

On top of all this, the van kept breaking down. I saw my hard-earned cash going into a piece of crap vehicle, and I wasn't happy about it.

"Not again," I moaned to John. "We should have bought Japanese, rather than a German vehicle."

"I know, I know. This isn't what I signed up for either. Let's just get it fixed and be on our merry way, shall we?" He tried to make light of the situation.

"Well, I'm not happy. And the fact that we're retaking a route I already did last year irks me. I don't like to repeat myself. It really bothers me, and I don't know why." John ignored this.

"Here's a garage." John pulled in and the French mechanic came out to look at the engine. While he fixed it, John and I sat in the café, having a snack and drink.

"I don't think this is working," I said between bites.

"It's not ideal. The van needs some work."

"Those Australians lied to us. And I don't like that."

"I don't know that they lied. Maybe they had better luck than we did."

"I don't believe they didn't know the van was in bad shape. It *had* to have broken down on them. It's old and dilapidated. It's disgusting."

"You have to admit, though, it's been nice not having to sleep in hotels."

"Yeah. I forget I'm in the Hilton." I glared at John,

remembering the cold nights in the van.

"You're in a foul mood." I felt John was right, and knew it was a sign I was ignoring my intuition that seemed to nag at me constantly.

"It seems to be the only mood I'm in these days." This trip still wasn't setting right with me, and the van breaking down had to be a sign of something.

"You're not *that* angry, I can tell. Just frustrated, as am I."

"I'm not happy. All I know is, I don't know if I can take much more of this." I quit eating. I was too upset.

"Let's see how we feel when we get to Spain."

"Fine." After a couple of hours, the van was supposedly ready to go. We got in and made our way down the coast of Spain.

And, of course, the next day the van broke down again. By this time, I'd had it. My last nerve was gone.

"I can't take this anymore," I yelled at John. "All of our money is going into this stupid heap of rubbish. I'm not spending another dime on it."

"I'm not happy with this either," he shouted back.

"Why do I let you talk me into these messes? You really don't know what you're doing sometimes, and it's annoying. We shouldn't have bought this van. And your friends are jerks for setting us up."

"Don't call my friends jerks."

"Jerks. Jerks!" I shouted out at him.

"Stop it. This is getting us nowhere. We're both upset."

"I'm not going anywhere in this van again. Especially with *you*."

"If that's how you feel, why don't you bugger off, then?"

That did it. My inner demon heard all of this and reared its head. I didn't belong here, or with John. It was time to move on. I pulled out our traveler's checks and handed him half; then, I picked up my backpack and stormed out of the van, slamming the passenger door as I went. I didn't turn around.

Eventually I found the train station and booked a ticket to Paris. I called the airline to see if I could fly home from there, instead of London, and they assured me I could.

As I waited for the train, a verse crept into my mind:

Should I stay, or should I go?

Inner Demon, let me know.

But I knew the inner demon wouldn't hesitate to leave. It had always been that way.

As I rode the train all night, I thought of my relationship with John. Sometimes it was too good to be true, and sometimes—like today--it was a nightmare. I questioned whether we were meant to be together or not. Maybe it was time to cut the string and forget it. It wasn't going to work after all and we weren't meant to be together. Soul contract or not.

As the train rolled along and I could hear the click-clack of the wheels, I stood in the hallway and lowered one of the windows. I closed my eyes and let the wind hit my face. It felt good. I reached down and touched the ring on my finger. The one I had loved so much. The one that didn't seem to work on me. I had tears in my eyes as I pulled it off my finger. I wondered what I was doing, but I threw it out the window anyway. I realized I was really letting John go, and that was probably a good thing. He was a victim of my youth.

I still loved John, but we would get over each other. It would take time. For now, freedom and not belonging with John were all I could think about. I closed my eyes and tried to sleep, even though I knew I wouldn't. Not for some time.

Lesson: Once you've let someone go, there's no going back. Not ever.

Chapter 23

I arrived in Miami to an empty house. I had no idea where my parents were, and I had not called to let them know I was returning. I called Gina at work, and she informed me that our parents had taken a short vacation to Central America.

"But I have a question. Did you and John have a fight?" she asked suddenly.

"Maybe. Why do you ask?" I felt tense and worried.

"He was calling Mom and Dad until they left a few days ago. So then he called me. He's worried about you and wants to know that you're okay."

"I'm fine."

"Yeah, right. You don't sound fine. Anyway, I have to get back to work. I'll see you soon." She hung up.

I decided to make some tea, hoping it might cheer me up. I'd never felt so miserable in my life. I couldn't believe what I just put myself through. I was pouring the tea when there was a knock on the door. I decided not to answer. I wasn't in the mood for company. But the knocking persisted, so I finally answered it. I opened the door to find John, looking as solemn and depressed as I felt. In spite of myself, I hugged him and kissed him, overjoyed that he was here.

"I don't know if you want me or not anymore, but I had to fly here to see you," he said softly in my ear.

"I'm glad to see you," I said back to him.

He came in and we had tea together on the living room sofa.

"How did you get here?" I asked suddenly.

"I drove your sister's car. She went to work with a friend."

"You stayed at my sister's place?" Gina doing this boggled my mind. And she said nothing about it.

"Yes, she was nice about it. She really can be great sometimes." He sipped his tea and put his hand on mine. "I thought you didn't want me anymore. Is that true?" he asked looking at me. I stared into his eyes. They always seemed to get to me.

"Well, you've traveled thousands of miles to be with me. That says a lot." I kissed him.

"I love you. You know that. You must know that, otherwise why would I come after you?"

"I know. I love you, too."

"I looked all over for you once you left the van. For hours. I thought you'd go to a park to cool down. When I couldn't find you I got really worried. Don't ever do that again, please."

"You don't know me very well. When you told me to bugger off, that set off alarms in my system. I don't do well with not belonging, and that's how I felt at that time. That

144

I didn't belong with you. And when that happens I'm out. I usually don't look back. And now you're here and my emotions are all wacky again."

"Please say you won't leave me again like that. I don't know if I can live without you." He put his arm around me, and then he looked at my bare finger. "What happened to the ring? Never mind, I don't want to know. And I'm okay with whatever you did. Seriously. I want you, not the ring." He held me close and we both had tears. We were emotional wrecks.

"I know I can't continue like this. I just can't. This long distance doesn't work and neither does being together all the time," I said between sobs.

"Do you still want to get married? I know I still do." He looked down into his lap, and then at me.

"I see two choices. Either we break up, or we get married and live here or in England for a while. And both of us need to work. I'm not going to support us. If you can live with that, then we'll get married. Otherwise, I'll drive you to the airport." I let John make the decision, even though I knew he wanted to get married, which is what he said.

And just like John, he'd brought over a couple of gifts. A cute, pink negligee and an album by Pink Floyd, entitled, 'Wish you Were Here'. I kissed him and thanked him. He was always sweet that way. I took the album as a sign that John wished I was with him, even after I left.

Had I known what was in store for me, however, I would have driven him to the airport and paid for his flight home. Never to be heard from or seen again.

Lesson: Be true to yourself or pay the consequences.

Chapter 23

My parents were surprised to see John and me at their home. They were glad we were making plans to get married, and felt that John would be making an honest woman of me. They never said that, but I could tell. They seemed less pleased about the nontraditional wedding we had planned, which would take place in a few months.

John and I walked along the Miami Beach, enjoying the surf, sky, and crying seagulls. We couldn't seem to decide where to get married. Suddenly, I spotted several beautiful palm trees off to the side, with grass and shade. I walked over to it, tugging John along with me. He protested at first, but then we stood there together, overlooking the ocean and feeling the breeze.

"This is a perfect place for a wedding. I know we didn't talk about the beach, but isn't this nice?" I looked at him for confirmation. He looked at me and then at the ocean.

"The best. It feels so peaceful here."

"We have a Justice of the Peace performing our ceremony. We have our marble cake with white icing. And I have my flowers picked out. All I need is a dress. And my parents are arranging the reception and photographer."

"I have to rent a tuxedo, too. But I can't believe we

found such a nice spot."

Of course my family took a different view, especially my sister.

"You're getting married on the beach? With all the sand and fleas?" Gina asked, putting her hand to her forehead. "You guys really are crazy."

"Yes. It's all the rage. Haven't you heard?" I replied.

"What song are you going to play for the first dance?" she asked. I looked at John, but he just shrugged.

"We haven't decided yet. But we will," I said finally.

"I hope you're flexible about your wedding date. We're looking at hotels and halls now. And music? I hope a deejay is okay." My mother was all aflutter with wedding plans. She couldn't stop talking about the various plans and worried things wouldn't be right. "We're flexible, Mom. Whatever works for you, and thank you for allowing John's parents to stay here. As well as Lyn and Roger."

"What about Lyn? When is she getting here?" my mother asked as she looked through wedding invitations.

"She'll be here tomorrow. And she's as excited as I am. Or maybe I'm just nervous."

"How can you be nervous? You're getting married on the beach and everything looks like a party rather than a wedding," said Gina. "I'm having a large traditional wedding when I get married."

"Of course. You don't care if you bore everyone. Trust me. Church weddings are boring," I said.

"Don't argue," Mom said, still writing invitations.

"Do you want help with the invitations? John and I can help you." I tried to change the subject.

"No, I'm fine. You guys should get your outfits, or you'll be going naked," she laughed at first, then looked worried. "You won't get married naked, will you?"

"Yes. Naked sounds good. Maybe the guests, too. How fun!" John said, laughing. I poked him.

Everything was going smoothly for a few days, until I got a phone call. It was Connor. He was in town and wanted to see me. My heart racing, I decided I wanted to see him too. Lyn tried to talk me out of it. When I wouldn't listen, she insisted on going with me and watching us from a distant table in the café.

"I don't want you doing anything you'll regret. I'm your maid of honor and I'm supposed to look after you." We talked outside on the patio near the pool, sipping lemonades. The umbrellas gave us shade from the hot Miami sun.

"I'm not going to do anything. I just want to talk to him," I insisted.

"You must really like him. You've been writing to him all this time. And John knows about him, which is good. Hopefully he won't hurt him. You've known him almost as long as John. Wow!"

"I'm not telling him until after the fact." I sipped my lemonade under the table umbrella, and watched the water in the pool.

"Tell me again what happened to your engagement ring?"

"It jumped out of a train window months ago. It committed suicide, or actually, I committed homicide. And there are days I wished I'd gone with it."

"Oh my! You two have the best drama. Ever since you met. But you really are perfect for each other. I was there when the romance started, so I know your history." She paused. "I can't believe it was almost two years ago. Time has flown. I have my own secret." She stared at me to get my attention.

"Do tell." I leaned in to hear.

"I got married in Paris a month ago to a French doctor. His name is Pierre St. Claire. I haven't told anyone. My parents will not be delighted about the news."

"Congratulations. They don't like foreigners?"

"Yes. They want me to marry a nice American guy. Like there are any! A few here and there, but European men are to die for. I plan on telling them soon."

"I totally agree. So are you coming with me to see Connor, or not?" I asked as I stood up.

"I wouldn't miss it for the world. I have to see this guy that's got you all hot and bothered." We laughed.

Connor sat at a table and stood up to greet me. He had recognized me immediately. I remembered his lovely face and manners. I felt relieved that he knew me. We hugged and kissed briefly.

"It's so good to see you again," he said. He had a glass of wine and I ordered one. "Do you want something to eat?" We couldn't take our eyes off each other. I wondered if I could elope with him.

"No. I'm good. It's so great to see you. What are you doing here in Miami?"

"I came to see you. It's been awhile, but you're always on my mind."

"I think about you at times, especially recently. But I have some news." I hesitated. I finally said, "I'm getting married in a week. And I can't believe I'm saying that."

"Really?" He looked surprised and hurt. I felt awful. I wanted to cry. I looked over and saw that Lyn was watching us. I looked away quickly.

"I'm so sorry. I have these feelings for you that I can't shake. But I'm committed to this relationship, I've been in for some time. We broke up briefly and now we're back together. The fact that we're actually getting married surprises me as well. I guess I thought it would never really happen."

"Why did you break up? Never mind. It's none of my business," he said, waving his hand like it didn't matter.

"I don't mind." I told him the story. The waiter brought my white wine.

"And you're still marrying this guy?" He seemed surprised.

"You think I shouldn't?" I asked and sipped my wine. Doubts about John started seeping in again, and I wondered if my intuition was trying to tell me something.

"Well, it's almost like something is telling you not to get married, right?"

"Yes. And yet I can't say no to a guy who flew thousands of miles to see me and still wants to marry me. We've been through a lot. And I do love him, for better or for worse." John had always felt like a soul mate and our connection so intense, it was hard to deny.

"Sounds like it. I've met some women in my travels, but always put you first. My mistake." He looked miserable again.

"I feel awful. How can I make it up to you?" I couldn't believe how my emotions were playing havoc with me.

"It's really okay." He touched my hand and looked at me. "If it wasn't meant to be, it wasn't meant to be. But I need to go now. I hope you both are happy and have a wonderful life together." He kissed my forehead and walked away. I watched him leave, and then Lyn came over to sit down in his chair. She touched my hand, but she didn't say anything.

"I'm a wreck! What am I doing?" I asked.

"Getting married to the man you love and who loves you. Dearly. No one is going to love you like John does. I see it in his eyes. And you *know* this."

"Then why do I feel so bad? Connor makes a point

about this fate thing. What are the chances of him showing up like this? At this time? I'd say a million-to-one."

"True. It's a strange coincidence. But so was meeting John in Paris, remember? Now let's go look at dresses, or you really will be getting married naked. Your poor mother. She would string you up alive, I swear. But I do like her and your dad. Your sister is okay, too. I can see where you two would butt heads. Really different personalities. But it's okay."

"Maybe looking at dresses will cheer me up, because right now I feel terrible."

I was thinking of what Jim said on the freighter, and wondering what my life would be like if I'd actually chosen a different reality. But then I remembered what John and I had been through all this time. A lot. And deep down, I knew I was making the right decision. At least I hoped so.

Lesson: When fate gives you a second chance, take it. The Universe is trying to tell you something.

Chapter 24

Like everything about the wedding, my dress looked like it was for a nice party, rather than a wedding. I liked it. The white dress and its blue trim fit my body tightly. It reached my toes and had slits on both sides. I could wear it again and again if I wanted to. I bought a white hat to keep the sun out of my eyes. My bouquet consisted of beautiful yellow colored roses, which reminded me of the rose John gave me in Paris.

Lyn bought a dress that matched mine, but in blue. She looked lovely. She thanked me for not choosing traditional dresses. "A waste of money," she proclaimed. We tried on our dresses in my room one more time.

"What did your Aunt Emma say about your wedding and Connor?" She put on her dress.

"She said it was a choice and that consequences will play out." I put on my shoes.

"Like karma? Or fate?"

"I guess. She didn't elaborate much. Almost like she didn't want to tell me too much. Which isn't like her at all. Very mysterious."

"I guess you'll know one day. Maybe your dream won't come true after all."

"Perhaps." I changed the subject. "I can't believe I'm getting married tomorrow. John is very calm about this wedding. I feel nervous."

"Wedding jitters. You'll get over it. And John picked a nice tuxedo. I'm surprised he went with it instead of a suit."

"I told him he could wear shorts or jeans, and I would be fine with it. But he likes his tuxedo."

"He wants to look as handsome as possible for you. He cut his hair some too. It looks better. What song did you guys pick?" She looked at me as she adjusted her dress.

"We have so many to choose from, but we picked 'Time after Time' by Cyndi Lauper."

"I like that one. It describes your relationship well. You've always been there for each other."

"How do I look?" I turned to her and put my hat on.

"Fabulous. Your skin is ravishing." As she said this, John walked in.

"Oh, sorry! You look so beautiful." He put my face in his hands and kissed me. "I've already seen your dress, so I don't think it's bad luck."

"I don't believe in that anyway," I replied. Lyn watched us.

"Do you wish you had eloped? Or gotten married in Greece?" she asked us.

"No. This is perfect for us," I said. "We have our marriage license and soon it will be official." John agreed.

My wedding jitters calmed down when I saw John in

his tuxedo, and he looked so relaxed. He squeezed my hand as if to say everything would be fine. It helped.

The day turned out perfect. The sun shone brightly and the palm leaves blew to remind me there really was a breeze. The waves pelted the sand, which you could hardly hear from the spot we picked. The seagulls cried out at times during our ceremony, making us smile. Uninvited guests watched our ceremony and took photos. I tried not to mind. I had no one to blame but myself for getting married in such a public place. After we kissed and signed our certificate, photos were taken. I was now Mrs. Shawna Fontaine, and it felt great.

Everyone had a good time. We laughed, danced, and kissed throughout the afternoon and evening. I danced with anyone and everyone, as did John.

Looking at our photos several days later, we talked about the minister and relived the experience.

Our favorite photograph turned out to be one from the beach. John sat on a bench and I sat on his knee. The trees and ocean in the photo seemed reminiscent of our life together. All thoughts of Connor were wiped from my mind, as I planned my life with this man that I'd met so long ago in Paris.

We honeymooned in the Keys, and as John swept me up over the threshold I remembered the numerous times he had done this. Our lovemaking had always been good and that night was no exception. John and I always seemed to know what the other desired without being told. Hearts and souls melted together, and the smoldering fire we built in Paris turned into a fiery mass of passion and love. It left us breathless and always wanting more.

"I'll never stop loving you. You know that, right?" he'd whisper in my ear.

"I know. I'll never stop as well." We couldn't believe our good fortune in finding each other.

But as usual, my dreams of a man dying while skydiving showed up that night. It seemed to get more prevalent as the days went on. As if taunting me about what a disastrous decision I'd made. Yet I still felt like I'd made the right decision. And only time would tell.

Lesson: Listen to your heart. Hear what it has to say and then make a decision. Hopefully the right one.

Chapter 25

John and I continued to live in Miami, much to my dismay. He wanted to experience the American way of life, and I didn't want to deny him that. And he kept his word about keeping a job, even if he didn't like it. If he didn't, he would find something else before quitting.

We found an apartment near the beach and committed ourselves to stay for six months before moving to Paris. We could both work there, and have a new and different lifestyle. John spoke French, and his family in France could help him get a good job. In the meantime, we worked, played, visited friends and my family, and reminisced about our past. But I was getting restless. The risk taker in me wanted to do something dangerous. I thought of skydiving and decided one day to go for it. I let John know, not expecting him to join me.

"I'm thinking of skydiving. It's something I've always wanted to do." I told him at breakfast.

"Really? It could be fun. I would like to try it as well. Where would we go?" I told him about the school not too far away, where we could learn the ins and outs. He seemed more enthusiastic than I imagined he would be. I didn't want him to do this, but there was nothing I could do once he'd decided. My parents did not share our enthusiasm.

"Do you two have a death wish?" asked my dad. He sat in his recliner and looked sternly at us. I'm sure he thought I was going along with John's idea.

"It's not John's idea. It's mine. I've wanted to do this for some time." I hoped I could talk John out of it after a jump or two. My dream made me anxious about his safety.

"I hope you two have life insurance. And your premiums will go sky high," Dad warned.

"I know. We have. And our wills are up to date. Not to worry," I reassured him.

"I hope you know what you're doing," said my mom, who was sitting on the sofa with us. Everyone was drinking coffee or tea. I almost wished I hadn't told them, but if I died I didn't want them too shocked about it. They could then say to my dead body, "*I told you so*", and my spirit would laugh from the other side, totally free and happy.

We discussed the procedure and the safety precautions in place. We bought the helmet, boots, and one-piece jumpsuit. We had taken the training, watched videos, and practiced jumps from a platform, and learned how to roll properly. We were as ready as we could be. I invited my parents to come out and watch us, but they declined. If I was going to die, they didn't want to watch it. I understood.

Gina came to visit and the whole conversation had to be repeated for her. She shook her head and put the blame on me.

"You always need excitement. There's something wrong with you, you know that?" she said after she heard the story. I knew it was just her fear coming through.

"Then there must be something wrong with me as well," said John, after sipping his tea.

"Don't talk to your sister like that!" said my dad, defending me.

"There's an element of truth to it. I don't like the same routine over and over. It's just the way I am. There's nothing wrong with adventure," I said looking directly at her. "More of it wouldn't hurt you."

She grimaced and said no more.

But that night in bed, John and I discussed our own beliefs and feelings about death.

"I believe we live on after death, but I have no proof. At least, not yet," I said leaning on my elbow and looking into his eyes.

"Me too. I believe in reincarnation. I really do. I suppose that's proof enough," he said, lying in the same position. "I believe you and I have met before."

"I agree. Are you afraid to die?" I asked.

"No. Not really. How about you?"

"Never. I feel like I've been ready for a long, long time," I snuggled into his waiting arms. "I think when we die we go to a better place. Whether it's another dimension, planet, star, or whatever. I know we talked about stars that night in Israel, and I still believe that."

"That we return to stars."

"You remember?"

"It struck home with me as well. Maybe we're from the same one."

"Could be true. But if we don't have harmonious relationships here with each other, we won't have them on the other side either. There has to be peace."

"I think that's true." John was quiet for a bit, then said, "If anything ever happens to me, I'll come and visit you." He looked at me closely. "Or at least I'll try."

"Where did that come from?" I stroked his hair gently and thought about my dream.

"I don't know. It's just a thought I've had, and now that we're skydiving, anything can happen."

"Maybe we have a death wish after all?" I asked. He kissed me.

"I don't think so. We just like adventure, and there's nothing wrong with that."

"So tomorrow we jump and hope for the best?"

"Something like that." We kissed good night and I lay in bed, remembering my dream. I knew the first jump would be more controlled than the ones after it. Still, I couldn't help thinking I was sending my husband on a suicide mission. One that I had initiated. I hardly slept at all.

Lesson: Enjoy your time with each other, and don't

take anything for granted.

Chapter 26

As I jumped from the plane, I felt excited, scared, and alive all at once. I was falling rapidly, just like in my dream, and I yelled enthusiastically. Once the chute opened I felt a sense of relief and looked around me. I saw the water in the distance, and the lush greenery. I looked down and pulled the toggles on either side of my chute, as the arrow below me pointed in one direction, then another. I was enjoying the gliding ride down and continued towards the target spot. I landed unceremoniously and got myself up. I'd made it. I didn't die after all.

Several people came over to help with the parachute, and I looked up to see John falling. I almost didn't want to look, but I kept my eyes peeled on him anyway. Suddenly, his parachute opened and I felt relief wash over me. My dream was not going to come true after all. John glided down and then landed further away from me. We ran to each other, and there were lots of hugs and kisses. We were both excited to talk about our experience.

"That was thrilling!" he exclaimed.

"Me too. What a rush!" We both started talking at once, first to each, then to the other jumpers.

By the time we arrived home, we were both determined to do it again. But I wondered if it was such a good idea. We sat in the living room with our drinks and talked about it.

"Are you sure?" I asked him, thinking about the dream again. "Now we can say we've done it."

"Maybe. Let's try it again and then see. It scared me, but I also felt excited." He sipped his beer.

"It's expensive. This is not a cheap hobby."

"I know. But we're both working and making money. We should be fine, don't you think?"

"Yes, but we're also moving to Paris. That's not cheap."

"We can stay with my relatives outside of Paris," he suggested. John's French relatives were nice. Several had even come to our wedding. But I'd learned my lesson about living with friends and relatives. It's never the best situation.

"No. We've stayed with other people before. Not fun. And they live too far from Paris. Maybe for the first week or so, but then I need to live in Paris. And by ourselves."

"Okay. What job have you lined up for yourself?"

"A computer programming job at one of the hospitals. Secretarial work will have to wait until my French is better."

"You understand my French," he grins.

"Yes, your French is easy to understand. Especially when you use your body." We both chuckled.

"Anyway, we have lots of things to think about. And my parents invited us to dinner if we survived our jumps, which we did. We can tell them we laughed in death's face," I said with a triumphant look.

"Your dad is going to give us a hard time about it. He's really concerned about you."

"That's because he still envisions me taking over his law practice. He knows Gina won't do it. Poor dad. No one wants to follow in his footsteps. Another disappointment," I said with a sigh.

"Life is full of disappointments, Shawna. The goal is not to have too many. Or at least try not to. Am I a disappointment to you?"

"Yeah, I'd say so. You're not rich. You're not that good looking. And you get moody. What's not to be disappointed about?" I laughed.

"So you're saying I'm not rich or that good looking?" He said sarcastically, then started to chase me. I squealed and ran to the bedroom, where he collapsed on top of me and began tickling.

"Hey, stop! Not fair," I shouted. I tried to tickle him back, but he grabbed my arms so I couldn't. Pretty soon we were in our usual frisky mood and our clothes came off way too easily. Obviously the parachute jumping had our endorphins running wild, or was it just the wildfire I felt all over my body every time John touched me? Our bodies melted and time stood still. I wondered if we would always feel this way about each other. Only time would tell. And a prediction or two about our future in Paris. Time to visit

Aunt Emma.

Lesson: Every moment in life counts. It either counts for you or against you. It's up to you which way the counting goes.

Chapter 27

I sat in Aunt Emma's kitchen while she made us some tea. She had an open floor plan, and I walked through the dining room and living room to the patio overlooking the ocean. I loved looking at the waves and smelling the sea salt. Seagulls and sandpipers fought over small bits of fish food on the beach. I sighed as I recalled how I tried to talk John out of skydiving this morning. I talked to the ocean about this, but all it did was wave at me. I realized that could be John waving goodbye, as he slowly descends to his death. I tried not to think about it. He could be so stubborn sometimes.

"Do you want to sit out here?" asked my aunt.

"Yes. That would be nice. It's shaded and it's a nice day," I sat on the white wicker chair. My aunt placed the teacups and teapot on the matching table.

"Didn't you miss the sunshine when you went traveling? There must have been places where it wasn't so sunny." She poured the tea.

"Austria, Switzerland, and Germany had plenty of sunshine, even though it was cold. But it was so beautiful I got lost in the snowcapped mountains. The people in Europe were so friendly. I will never forget their hospitality and generosity to strangers. That warmth makes up for any foul weather." I remembered hitchhiking in the rain. Brutal.

"You've had quite an adventure. And more to come." She winked at me. "And John is jumping today, I guess. You can only guide someone. You can't control or change them."

"I think you can influence someone, and it can be positive or negative." I sipped my tea and looked at the tea leaves floating around in my cup. I slid my sunglasses on top of my head.

"I know you don't do this, but some people try to control others because they can. They take advantage. Emotional blackmail even. You're so freedom-loving that you would never do that, but not everyone is like you. Remember that." She sipped her tea and looked out at the ocean

"Is there a reason you're telling me this?"

"Not really. Just a gentle reminder to let John do skydiving, and not let your dream influence you. Whatever happens will happen. No matter what."

"Right. I couldn't stop him once he decided to join me."

"He doesn't want me to read for him, does he?" she asked intently.

"No. I think he's afraid of what you'll say."

"He should be. I see some things. Besides the dream, are you picking up anything else?"

"Nothing specific."

"It's probably just as well. Are you almost done?"

"Yes." I turned the cup over into the saucer and handed it to her.

"Let's see. As you know, anything near the lip of the cup will happen soon. And you know that anything you don't like to hear, you can change."

I nod.

"Okay. There's the Eiffel Tower in here. And looks like in a couple of months you'll be going there. Is that true?"

"Yes. We haven't told anyone yet. Don't say anything to my parents yet, please."

"Everything between us is confidential. My word is sacred."

"Right. I know that. You've kept many a secret."

"There's a letter T in your cup. Looks female and someone you know. I also see two other people you know with initials L and P. There's a man skydiving. So looks like John takes his new hobby to heart. He works in an office, but doesn't necessarily like it. He likes the money, though." Emma looked at me. "He just hasn't found his niche has he?"

"No. It's been frustrating at times. He lives for today and doesn't worry about tomorrow. I worry enough for both of us."

"You're job looks solid. You'll never have to worry about that. Jobs seem to find you." She gave me a knowing smile. "Well this is interesting. It looks like a veil. Like it's being drawn down so I can't see. Something is being hidden from you. I don't get this very often. It usually means trickery, sneakiness." As she said this, her cup started to shake in her hands, like it had all of a sudden come alive. I stared in disbelief and looked at her face. She'd lost all color and seemed to be in a trance. I wanted to touch her and get her out of it, but decided not to. Suddenly the cup jumped from her hands and crashed to pieces on the patio. The sound startled her and she gasped.

"Are you alright?" I asked, touching her hands, which were now empty, but still shaking a bit.

"I will be. Give me a minute." She closed her eyes.

I bent down and started picking up the pieces of the cup. Tea leaves were splashed everywhere. One group looked like Tower Bridge, but one group caught my eye. As I looked at it closely, it seemed to be a face. I couldn't tell if it was male or female, but it had slits for eyes and mouth. I tried to get closer still, when my aunt's foot tapped it and it disappeared.

I quickly picked everything up and went to get a broom and dustpan. My aunt looked at me and smiled a little.

"I'll take care of everything. You just relax." I went inside and came back out. I cleaned everything up. When I came back out I found her standing at the edge of the patio; she was staring at the ocean.

She turned and looked at me. Color had come back

into her face and she appeared calm.

"I don't know what happened there. But there was definitely an unknown entity around. You have a lot of protection around you. Make sure white light surrounds you at all times. Be very careful of the future you're stepping into. Some of it is a problem. I don't like it. I don't like it at all."

"I'll change it."

"Yes. Some of it, you might be able to. You can always try." She didn't sound convincing.

"You don't know what it is?"

"No. But veils are not a good sign. Just be careful and try not to be too concerned about anything."

"You know that won't happen." We both smiled. I hugged her tightly. What would I do without her?

I knew I liked to live in the fast lane. Perhaps I would have to move over to the slow lane for a while. No. That would not be me. And besides, Paris was waiting for us.

Lesson: Always protect yourself. And when a psychic warns you, pay extra close attention.

Chapter 28

After six months in Miami, we flew to Paris. I melted into the flame of Paris all over again. It seemed like we had never left; yet it was a new adventure, since neither of us had lived there. We were excited and anxious at the same time.

"This is where we met so long ago now," said John as we settled into our apartment on the Left Bank, which his relatives had found for us. We sat on our sofa, admiring our small apartment.

"I can't believe it's been over two and a half years since we were last here. And our apartment is small, but lovely," I looked at John and kissed him. Another chapter in our lives.

My French improved, and I loved the language. Our jobs turned out to be better than we had hoped. The Europeans had a more relaxed lifestyle that I had difficulty getting used to. My coworkers teased me about my hyper mode, and soon I slowed down. It made them less tense. And John liked his job, even though it wasn't ideal. After three months, he thought he might be able to stay there much longer.

He still skydived and I joined him sometimes, but for me the thrill of jumping was gone. I looked for other endeavors so Lyn and I took up hang-gliding, which I liked better. I thought it would be similar to skydiving, but this seemed a lot scarier. We had learned from pros, but it still felt like I was running to my death when I had to throw myself over the cliff. I could have sworn I felt shock waves run through my body and land firmly in my feet. Electric waves blasted through to my feet, then to the top of my head as I flew. I remembered flying. It's what I do best. I soared like a bird and loved looking at the scenery. My only wish is that I could have floated way up into the clouds instead of having to descend. I loved it. When I landed, I couldn't wait to try it again. Lyn felt the same way as we hugged and jumped up and down. It had to be the most death defying moment of my life. And soon this became one of our favorite pastimes. But now John was trying to talk me out of it.

"It's dangerous. More so than skydiving," he said, after my venture. We were in the living room having snacks and drinks.

"Maybe so. It's another thing I've wanted to do. I only dreamed of it a couple of times, so I'm honoring that dream." I grabbed some pretzels. "Besides, why should you have all the fun?" I leaned over and kissed him.

"Fine. But I'm against it. Just so you know. If something happened to you, I don't know what I would do."

"You'd go on living. What else is there to do?" I took a

176

sip of water.

"I might not want to." He took my hand and squeezed it. He looked despondent when we looked at each other.

"You'd have no choice. Besides you're probably going to go before me." I wanted to take that statement back as soon as I said it.

"Why do you say that? Do you know something I don't?" He looked at me intently.

"Women live longer than men. We're stronger, so it only makes sense. Besides if you were so concerned about dying, you'd quit jumping. And I don't see you doing that." I looked back at him.

"Okay. I'll buy that. Our anniversary is coming up soon. What do you want to do?" He was still holding my hand.

"Surprise me. I'll think of something for you. Not sure what it will be yet. We have a couple of months yet." I couldn't believe we'd just celebrated another Christmas together. Time was flying by. I already had John's gift planned. I had bought some guitar lessons for him. He still played at times, but not like he used to, and I didn't want him to give up his dream so easily. Sure, he still serenaded me once in a while, but I saw the sad way he looked at his guitar: like it was a childhood toy that had to be put away because he had gotten older.

On the day of our anniversary John had a surprise.

I had to keep my eyes closed while we took a taxi

177

somewhere. John guided me along the sidewalk. I had no idea where we were. We could have been in China for all I knew. Finally we stopped.

"You can open your eyes now," said John.

I opened my eyes and was startled. "Oh my goodness. We're at the abandoned youth hostel where we had spent our first night together. The first of many. I clapped my hands and we kissed.

"This is fabulous. What a great present." We wandered around the room, recalling our days of old. The youth hostel had gotten even more run down, but otherwise it looked the same.

"We're not sleeping here tonight. I don't care what you say." I said looking at John wildly.

"Of course not. Unless you really want to." He laughed and I joined him.

"No way. One night was enough. And I still remember it well. You're full of surprises." We walked hand in hand now throughout the whole building. I sat down on the spot where I had made my bed and John did the same. We looked at each other in silence. Our meeting seemed to have taken place so long ago.

"We've traveled a lot of miles together," said John breaking the silence.

"Yes, we have. And to think we almost broke up for good once. I can't even imagine that now." I shook my head.

John then came over and sat beside me. He put his arm around me and pulled me close to him.

"Just remember this. My life started with you and ends with you. Always." He held me tight, like I might disappear. I shivered, knowing that time works in mysterious ways. We're given paths and choices and have to make the proper decisions. Sometimes our lives depend on it.

"I really like the gift you gave me. I know you want me to play the guitar more and improve. I just don't know if I can. My heart's not always in it."

"And you look so heartbroken when you say that. Music is in your soul. Don't give up on it just because you think you're not good enough. You just have to keep practicing. Maybe these lessons will rekindle the fire you have for it. Which you still have."

"Maybe you're right. I'm not into earning money like you are. So in a couple of weeks I plan on quitting my job. And I know you don't like that."

"What will you do?" I'd been glad he lasted as long as he did. Six months at one job was a milestone.

"I have a job lined up at a music store. See, I haven't totally given up my dream." He smiled at me to brighten the occasion.

"Good. I guess we can still afford the apartment, but we'll have to take it easy on other things. I guess that could work. Perhaps we should move to London. It seems like a better choice. We've talked about it and both of us miss it. Not that I don't like Paris. But for me, London feels more like home."

"Me too. Maybe in a couple of months."

"Maybe you should rethink quitting your job, since we'll be moving anyway."

"It's hard to be there. But since there is an ending, I'll think about it."

We got up to leave, and I brushed a little dirt off of my pants. John did the same.

"I'm not disappointed we got married, you know. In fact I'm glad we did. I always wanted to marry you." John said this as we walked out, hand in hand.

"I'm glad I married you, too. I love you," I said. We kissed for a long time.

"I love you, too. Always and forever. When I met you I felt like I'd always known you. Strange, but true." He hugged me.

"I know what you mean. I felt the same way." As we walked to the restaurant to celebrate, John said we would go to the top of the Eiffel Tower as well.

As we kissed and looked out at the beautiful lights of Paris, John looked into my eyes.

"The lights in your eyes look like stars. And they always beckon me home. I love that."

"So do your eyes, John," I whispered. "So do your eyes."

Lesson: Money doesn't buy happiness, but it sure gives you a lot of opportunities and freedom…freedom to go wherever you want.

Chapter 29

Four months after our anniversary, John started acting strange. He became moody, irritable over little things, and picked fights with me for no reason. I thought he was possessed, because he just wasn't himself. Even the guitar lessons I bought him drove him crazy. He didn't want to go to them, and said they were a waste of money. I offered to go skydiving with him and he freaked out. He didn't think I should go, as it wouldn't be any fun for me. He found new Australian friends, Shelly and Bruce, and we hung out with them regularly. He seemed happy when we were around them. I was glad he found new friends, but he seemed obsessed with them and what they were doing. Our finances weren't in the best state, so I gave up my hang-gliding to save money for London.

"They're only here for a couple of months, and then they start traveling. I want to enjoy my time with them," he said to me as we ate dinner one night. I wondered what John had gotten himself into. Thank goodness I had control over our finances, or we might have been broke, as he spent so much time and money with these people. Shelly and Bruce were not bad people, but something definitely wasn't right.

"Fine. We can go to this party. Where is it?" I asked, eating my salad.

"It's in a pub. Very casual. I know you think they're a bad influence, but they're not," he said this as if reading my mind. I was beginning to think that he could. We had always had that kind of rapport with each other, but lately even that was all over the place.

"Okay. Sounds good." I looked away.

"I know you're not happy about this. You don't have to go if you don't want to, but I wish you would." After pushing me away for a couple of weeks, now he wanted me to go. I wished John would make up his mind.

"I'll go. It might actually be fun," I said, knowing John likes pubs and drinking more than I did. He always seemed to need people around him, and didn't like spending a lot of time by himself. I often wondered if he was afraid of his own thoughts or feelings, yet he could have profound wisdom sometimes from out of nowhere. He could certainly be mysterious at times.

The pub was noisy, with rock-and-roll music blasting. There were about nine of us around a table, and I could barely hear what was being said. I was introduced to everyone, even though I knew most of the guests. And then it happened. A woman with long, dark hair joined us. She sat across from John and introduced herself to me.

"I'm Marta," she said to me. We didn't shake hands, and I noticed that she and John seemed to know each other.

"We met once before. I'll get drinks for us." And with

that, John was gone rather quickly.

I looked at the woman and my body went into high alert. Red flags everywhere. I hated her and glared at her. She tried not to look at me and glanced at our table companions, who were busy talking. I saw through her, and right to her soul I went. It was dark and evil. Someone I could not trust, and someone John should not be trusting, either. She might be able to fool John, but she could not fool me. I had my suspicions about her but kept them to myself. Now I felt I really knew what was going on with John. My tense body would not relax around her. Drinks were not helping, as I watched her trying to flirt with John in front of me. She acted so coy. She was not very pretty, and I wondered what he saw in her. She was average and did not have integrity. At least none that I could see. John and I left early, and I questioned him when we got home.

"So who is she really?" I asked angrily. I threw my purse on the table as I said this. I knew my eyes were glaring at John, but I didn't care. I wanted answers.

"No one. I met her a couple of weeks ago through Shelly and Bruce," he looked at me and then looked away. "Do we need to talk about this now?" He turned to walk away, but I followed him.

"What's going on with you two?" Now my arms were crossed and I stared at him.

"Where is that coming from?" He looked at me from

across the room.

"You tell me. I know my intuition is accurate. Why would I hate someone I've never met before?" I kept my stance.

"I don't know. But nothing is going on, okay?" John looked uncomfortable.

But I knew something was going on. John would not look at me. He had never lied to me before, but now it appeared that he was.

"Well, it certainly explains your behavior lately. All that moodiness, petty nitpicking, and not wanting me to go places with you. Obviously you're having an affair with her. And I don't know why."

John would not answer. He said he was done talking and just wanted to sleep. I wondered how he could sleep with two women at the same time. He could try to lie all he wanted, but he wasn't fooling me. I met Lyn the next day for lunch.

"I think John's having an affair. And she's an evil person," I said after we ordered.

"John? Are you sure? It's not like him. I don't think he could stomach it. He's too sensitive about things like that. And why would he want the two of you to meet?" she pelted me with questions.

"I stand by what I saw. And why would I hate someone I've never met. Plus I want her to die. I really do. I could easily kill her, so that tells you something," I said in a hard voice. I thought of Sam's brother and wondered which one I wanted dead more. One phone call and both of them would be gone. Forget morals and the spiritual path. What good did that do me?

"Okay. I've never seen you like this. Let's be rational. And promise me you won't kill her, or John." She reached over and patted my hand. "I can see you're really angry. Let's order a drink, shall we?" Lyn called over the waiter and ordered a bottle of wine, then turned back to me.

"Describe her to me."

I gave her a description. Medium height and weight. Long dark hair and eyes, with a malicious demeanor. A narcissistic person if there ever was one. "There's absolutely nothing special about this person. Not one thing that I can say like, 'Oh yeah, she's so beautiful, great personality, rich, or whatever.' So of course I wonder what he sees in her." But then I wonder to myself what does she see in him?

"Okay, so nothing great. Why would John be attracted to someone like that?"

"You got me. I have no clue. None."

"But you don't know for sure."

I cocked my head to one side and sighed.

"Okay, he's denying it. Not the best thing he could be doing. How's your sex life? If you don't want to tell me, that's fine." The waiter arrived and poured our wine for us before I could answer.

"To friendship," I said as we lifted our glasses in a toast.

"To friendship, and may we always be friends." We clinked our glasses and gook a couple of sips.

"Our sex life is good like it always is. That's why this is so surprising. But I felt something was up, and seeing her made me realize exactly what it was. I think she wanted to see me, because John sure wouldn't have wanted that. She wanted to see her competition."

"Yeah, that seems right. The question is why would he go along with it? Keep the two women apart as much as possible. I'll have to ask Pierre. He's a guy and knows their egos. Thank goodness he's not like that."

"I never thought John would be like that either," I said, finishing off my wine.

"Is she French?" Lyn poured another glass for herself and me.

"No. From the conversation I overheard, she's from South America and is part French. She's studying art here, or something like that." I thought of them living in poverty, which is pretty much where they were headed.

"This wine is great. And I'm whining today." We both laughed. It felt good to talk to Lyn. But I knew deep down my suspicions were right.

Lesson: Dishonesty starts with the self. The lies you tell yourself to protect your feelings, and become a victim of them.

Chapter 30

For a few weeks, the tension hung between John and I like thunder that was ready to roar but couldn't. I observed John very closely and he was aware of it. I was asking too many questions about this other person and he didn't want to answer them. I told him I didn't believe him, when he said that nothing was happening with Marta. He had always been forthright and now he appeared to have shut down, and my intuition was still on high alert. I couldn't shut it down. Dreams about the situation haunted me. Three women talked to me and told me that I knew the truth. I answered, "*My husband is sleeping with this woman.*" They said yes, but then they taunted me. "*Do you know why he is sleeping with her?*"

"*No. I don't. Does he love her?*"

"*No. That's not it. Although, he might think that. Keep guessing.*"

"*She's using him? But if so, I don't know why.*"

"*You'll know years down the road. It can't be revealed until then.*"

"*Why?*"

"*We don't know. It's hidden. She blocks it from view. She knows it can get changed back.*"

"*What gets changed back? She turns back into a toad. I'm sure of it.*"

189

"*No. Something else.*" And then they disappear.

I would wake up confused over the dream. Someone or something was trying to give me important information.

One day, when John went to get some groceries, I looked for nail clippers in his top drawer. Lo and behold. What did I find underneath a book? Photos of Marta. Posing outside. It looked like the skydiving grounds. Of course. That explained him not wanting me to go with him. I looked through the six photos and picked one out. My heart was racing and I was getting angry. I glared at the photo and wished I could kill her with my eyes. I tore it up and put the pieces on the bed for John to see when he returned. As I waited for him to get back, I grew more enraged. Now I wanted to kill him and wondered why I hadn't bought a gun a long time ago. French prison couldn't be that bad, could it? Freedom. I needed freedom. I pushed aside the gun and homicidal thoughts. For now.

By the time John got home, I was in full Gorilla mode and all I wanted to do was tear him to pieces.

"Come here, John," I yelled out from the bedroom doorway. "I need to show you something."

He set down the groceries and walked in. He noticed the photo pieces on the bed.

"What the hell is going on? And don't lie to me." I yelled.

He looked relieved and distressed at the same time. I didn't feel sorry for him.

"Okay." He sat on the end of the bed and looked down at the floor. He wouldn't look at me. "I've been with her. Just a couple of times."

"In other words, you're sleeping with her. And she's fine sleeping with a married man?" I say still fuming.

"She didn't agree with it at first."

"Oh, and now she's okay with it. Because you said it was? Why are you doing this?"

"I don't know. I'm totally confused right now." He put his head in his hands and covered his eyes.

"You're an asshole. You know that?" I wanted to hit him, but I didn't do it. I couldn't believe I had some control left in my body, which was shaking with rage.

"I know. You don't have to tell me."

"What do you see in her? She's not that pretty. Seriously?"

"I don't know. I wish I could explain it," John said quietly now. He looked so ashamed of himself as he glanced up at me. He knew he had caused me pain. But what I didn't know was how much pain and hurt he had caused to himself.

"Do you want a divorce?" I asked.

"No. I don't think so."

"Do you love her?"

"Not really. I can't explain." As usual when confronted with his behavior, John became vague. "This is against my nature to do this."

"So why are you doing it? You know she's using you, right?" Now he looks even more confused. "You think you're using her and feel guilty about that. But she's really a con artist and you can't see it."

"I don't think she's like that," he said slowly, defending this awful person.

"Why? Because you can't admit you're wrong. That's always been a problem for you. Always."

"Well, maybe I was wrong marrying you," he said to me angrily.

"Maybe you were. I know I sure was," I said quietly. I finally calmed down. I knew deep down that I didn't want this man anymore. Not this one. Not the liar, adulterer, and deceiver sitting on the bed.

"I think you should go." I now had tears running down my face. I can't believe I married this horrid person. And I'd sacrificed Connor, who seemed like such a better man.

Now John looked at me with tears in his eyes. We hugged and cried together. I couldn't believe this was happening to us. John didn't want to go. He continued to say he loved me and that we were meant to be together. And like the fool I am, I believed him.

Lesson: Nice women don't sleep with married men. And married men who cheat deserve to die. But karma doesn't always happen overnight.

Chapter 31

John and I tried to make things work, but I couldn't trust him anymore. I became suspicious every time I wasn't with him. He refused to go to counseling, and wouldn't tell me what was wrong. He had no excuses for his behavior. He became moodier, and so after a week or two, I finally said I was moving to London with or without him. He didn't want me to go, but he didn't want me to stay either. In the end, he decided to move out and be with the evil one, as I had come to refer to Marta. I wasn't surprised. He had changed, and *not* in a good way. He was nothing like the man I met years ago and married. His ego had taken over, and once that happens there is no reasoning with an insane person. I knew John wasn't happy with himself, so how could he be happy with someone else? I also knew his sensitive nature and conscience would haunt him about this decision. But it was his cross to bear. And like his relationship with Natalie, there was no ending that could resolve the situation. I would be a force in John's new relationship. Why could he not learn from his mistakes?

John had forgotten his guitar on departure, so a couple of days before leaving for London, I sat down on the bed with it. I held it close to me. I thought of John as I strummed a few chords and hoped the music I played would reach him. If only I could remember the chords that John and I had sung together. Then he might remember his way back home. The music was forlorn, and as the guitar wept, I eventually joined it. It was a sad reminder of what our lives once were. The song was gone.

I was still packing, when Lyn and Pierre showed up to take me out to dinner.

"I can't believe you're finally leaving Paris," she said as we looked at the menu.

"London's calling me. And it's my home now. Or at least it feels like it." I ordered salad and vegetables.

"Are you a vegetarian now?" she asked. I nodded. "I think it's a good idea. I'm becoming one as well."

"I don't know if I can," said Pierre. He ordered a filet mignon medium rare, and I flinched at him. "Sorry. How are you holding up by the way? You look good."

"Numb. Paralyzed, maybe. But I'll survive. This might turn out to be the best thing that ever happened to me." Pierre poured me a glass of wine, then Lyn.

Lyn ordered a salad and vegetables as well. "I can always have desert if I'm still hungry. And you're right. Probably something great will come out of this for you. How's that skydiving dream lately?"

"I'm not having it as much." I explained my dream to Pierre, who looked impressed.

"Well, if that comes true, I think revenge is yours. Not that revenge is what you want," he added carefully.

"Sure it is. I want him dead. After the pain he caused, even death is too good. He should be tortured," I said, sipping wine. Pierre and Lyn exchanged glances.

"The good news is you get to start a new life in London. Not a bad thing. We could all use a clean slate once in a while," she sipped her wine as our salads arrived.

"I am going to miss hang-gliding. I guess I can do that in England, too. I will try that."

"It really is a dangerous sport. You might want to rethink it," Pierre said. Lyn had stopped a month ago due to Pierre's concerns. He didn't want to be a widower.

"I'll think about it. I have a long lifeline on my palm, so I'm not so worried," I explained between bites. "Dying is not the worst thing that can happen to someone."

"John has a short lifeline, if I remember. Doesn't bode well, along with your dream," Lyn took a bite of salad and added more olive oil.

"Does he believe in reincarnation?" Pierre asked, eyeing me closely.

"Yes, he does, or did. I don't know what he believes anymore since he's changed so much."

"Oh, that's not good," Pierre said. "I know men. And if he's changing for her, it's only a matter of time before *that* comes back to torment him. Plus all the lies and deceit they have to tell others and themselves. It's no way to live. Did he say he wanted a divorce?" He sipped his wine.

"No. Never mentioned it. As usual, it'll be up to me to

file all the paperwork. What he doesn't know is I'm not doing it. I figure if he really loves her and wants to be with her, he can prove it by getting the divorce and marrying her. We'll see if *that* ever happens."

"You sound so sure of this," said Lyn, sitting back in her chair and looking at me.

"I'm positive. When has John ever taken the path of resistance? He always takes the easy path. I bet one hundred dollars he never divorces me." Pierre thought he would, but Lyn agreed with me. She then added, "But I'll bet you'd file papers if Connor showed back up."

"You're right. I would. In a manic London second I would." The thought of Connor wanted to make me cry. What a mistake I'd made. A horrible, horrible mistake.

"Don't beat yourself up about Connor. There were no signs or indications John would act like this. Not ever. He just wasn't the type. I'm sure he told you that," Lyn looked at me, totally convinced of herself.

"You're right. We met lots of women in our travels and in Miami. Some who flaunted their bodies at him and he didn't pay much attention. He always said he could look, but couldn't touch. So much for that lie." The wine was making an impact on me. And my plate of vegetables had arrived.

"When's the last time you had a good reading?" Lyn dived into her veggies as well. I couldn't look at the steak Pierre was cutting. I almost felt nauseated.

"I'm going to cover this with potatoes and veggies so you can't see it." He smiled at me.

"Thanks. You're so nice, but don't ever cheat on my friend here." I turned to Lyn and said, "It's been a long time since I've had a reading. That's the problem. Surely someone could have foreseen this." I thought of my aunt's reading with the veils, but didn't know what it meant. Marta was hiding something that's for sure.

"I'm not like that. I'm strong-willed. But above all, I know myself. I couldn't live with myself if I cheated. Besides, some men have low self-esteem. Probably the woman he picked does, too. So it's all about ego. A crappy little fellow if there ever was one," said Pierre enjoying his steak.

"The good news is your life can only get better. It has to go up from now on," Lyn said, lifting her wine glass for a final toast. "Say goodbye to Paris and hope she redeems herself."

Lesson: You can always accept someone's flaws, but betrayal cuts to the bone. And there's no bandage. None.

Chapter 32

I meditated in my Paris apartment the day before leaving for London.

Hurricane John had picked me up and tossed me around high in the air, and then pounded me on the sand. Like my aunt's tea cup, I broke into pieces and lay at the bottom of the ocean. I wished sharks would eat me, but none came. But there was a gentle manatee that floated by and pushed all of my pieces together with her nose. Slowly, I became whole again. I found a shield and an arrow lying on the ocean floor, and quickly picked them up. I climbed on top of the manatee, and she easily carried me to the surface. I walked out of the water with my treasures and lay in the warm sun letting it heal my wounds. I closed my eyes for a time.

When I opened them an eagle was hovering above me, staring at me. I realized its message of freedom and strength, and soaring to new heights. I would be happy with or without John. I really did not need him. I never did. A connection to the divine was at hand and I needed to prepare. Change would be coming, and I welcomed it with open arms.

London. Home again. I felt like I could breathe once more. My new life had begun and I waited for the stirrings of new growth to move me onward and upward. No more going backwards ever again, I swore to myself.

I moved in with Trina. We became friends when I worked in London. A successful lawyer with room to spare for a lost American gal. But not for long, I hoped.

I wanted to meet a man to go out with, and as usual London provided for me.

I met Mark at a law firm I was temping at. He was good-looking, athletic, and blond, with blue eyes that had fun in them. I was attracted to him almost immediately. He joked with me, then asked the dreaded question.

"So, are you dating anyone?" He sat in the chair in the lounge after his appointment.

"Actually I'm married, but my husband's in a coma. And I have no idea where he is or when he'll wake up. It's a mystery." I smiled when I said it. He seemed amused.

"A woman who's neither married nor single? Quite the predicament, wouldn't you say?" His smile was beautiful.

"Yes. It is. I'm looking for fun with no strings attached. None." I said the last part firmly.

"I can understand that. Me too. I date a lot, but nothing serious. Women get kind of, oh, you know, clingy, perhaps."

"Then you wouldn't like my husband. He's very clingy. He just doesn't care *who* he clings to. That's the problem." I smiled and he returned it with an understanding look in his eyes.

"One of those. Yes, I understand. Not sure of themselves. So do you want to go out tonight?"

"I thought you'd never ask." I gave him my phone number and he gave me his card. He worked as a financial consultant. Mark Spencer. For All Your Financial Needs. The card was white with gold borders. Very posh.

"I'll pick you up at six, if that works for you?"

"Sounds good." I watched him leave, and for the first time in a long time, I felt excited. I hadn't dated in over three-and-a-half years. And I was going to have fun—lots of it.

I was on Cloud Nine and dancing around the apartment when Trina came in. Her long reddish blonde hair had gotten a little damp from the rain. Her gorgeous face beamed when she saw me in such an enthusiastic mood.

"I have to tell someone. I'm going on a date tonight. And I can hardly wait." I danced about the living room as I had so much energy.

"Who's the guy?" she asked. I told her. She opened her mouth and gasped. I stopped dancing and stood still.

"What is it?" I didn't like how she was looking at me so seriously.

"Not Mark Spencer in financial?" She walked over to me with determination.

"Yes. What about that?" I froze. Obviously bad news was coming. I hate bad news.

"He's kind of a womanizer. Very wealthy. Doesn't need to work, but he does. He has a plane that he flies some of his dates in. Usually dinner in Paris or Rome, or wherever. Also, he has boats and who knows what else. He definitely lives the high life."

"How do you know all this?"

"He's been written up in several journals. And my boss knows him. He tends to date models, but I believe that changed a couple of years ago. Don't know why."

"I must be a change as well," I eyed my clothes and body, which looked great, but not model material. A size five is still too big for a model.

"He's a nice guy, otherwise. He's been known to date all sorts of women. You're attractive. And he does like petite blondes," she eyed me over as she said this.

"I'd better dress up. He said casual on the phone."

"Then dress casual. I wouldn't change who you are for him. He likes genuine women. At least that's what I hear."

"Okay. I'll change into new jeans and a long-sleeved white sweater with nice gold trimming on the front. If he doesn't like it, I'll change."

By the time Mark showed up, I was a wreck. I tried several outfits and then went back to the jeans. I wished Trina had never told me about him. Party pooper.

I invited him in, and he handed me a flower. A red rose with a strong smell. I thought of the yellow rose John had given me years ago. I hoped this wasn't a premonition of things to come.

"Thank you. It's lovely," I said and invited him in. While I put the rose in water, I introduced Mark and Trina. They'd heard of each other, but never met. Trina's law firm was well known.

"I've heard a lot about you," Trina said to Mark, as my eyes opened wide and I shook my head. She ignored my hints.

"I hope you heard good things." He smiled, but a worried look crossed his face.

"Most of it. I hope you treat my friend right." Trina said, looking like she was interrogating a witness.

"I have no intention of hurting anyone. That's not in my personality." He looked at Trina with a flat affect, and waved his hand as if brushing off a hair.

I picked up tension between them, and suggested we leave before Trina sued him.

As we got to the curb, I stopped and stared. Surely we weren't driving in the car I was staring at.

"Get in," said Mark as he held open the door of the black Rolls Royce. I looked down at my clothes and realized I was underdressed. I hesitated. "What's wrong?" he asked.

"I think we're not dressed up enough."

"It's alright. Get in. I've worn worse clothes than these. She really can't see you." He smiled at me and, I got in the car. I felt like I was in heaven. Luxury and opulence didn't even begin to describe the inside of the car. I felt like a queen. The seats were plush and I nestled into them, hoping I would never have to leave.

"This is a beautiful car. I love it," I said excitedly, looking at Mark. He was so nonchalant about it. But of course, he grew up in an esteemed family. He was used to living an extraordinary life.

"I've had it for about six months. I bought it from a famous musician. And I won't tell you who it is." He grinned at me.

I tried to guess who it might be, but he wouldn't say. A man so full of secrets, that he wouldn't even tell me where we were going. He asked if I knew where we were, and I told him no. He grinned at that, and I felt grateful that he wasn't a serial killer. At least I hoped not.

We took the freeway south and the car drove smoothly. It felt like I was in a living room chair riding along the highway. We eventually end up at a beautiful estate, and Mark explained to me that an American had bought the place, and now hosted a private club there. You must own a Rolls Royce or a Bentley to belong.

The large Tudor house had several long, one story buildings nearby. It sat on several acres of land. I couldn't even imagine what the cost of it would be. Obviously millions of dollars.

"Very exclusive," he said, as we disembarked from the car. I nodded still in awe of the whole place. It looked like something you would see in British movies. And to ride up in a Rolls Royce! I felt privileged.

Inside we met our host, a tall, middle-aged American fellow with brown hair and eyes. He wore glasses, jeans, and a pullover. He was introduced to me as Mr. Edwards, and he loved everything about Britain. He sat us at a table and brought us some wine.

"It feels like a British pub in here," I said, looking around at the bar atmosphere. The windows looked out to a rolling hillside. "Where are we?" I tried to remember the signs along the way.

"Southwest London. A little outside of town. Do you want something to eat?"

"Sure. I'm vegetarian though, so maybe a salad with tofu or an egg."

"A salad sounds good." We ordered and I looked around to see some famous people. I mentioned this to Mark.

"If you promise not to get all crazy over them, I'll introduce you to one or two of them after dinner."

"I promise, I promise," I said excitedly. "I want to meet them." I could hardly eat now.

"The British value their privacy and don't like to be disturbed, but I know several. We'll join them later on."

However, we didn't have to wait until our meal was finished. A famous couple walked over and said hello to Mark, who introduced me to them. Outwardly I appeared calm, but my insides were shaking like a Chihuahua and screaming like a monkey.

When we left the building, I jumped up and down and did cartwheels across the lawn. Mark laughed. "I've never met a woman like you before. You're hilarious," he said.

I flew home in the Rolls Royce and never touched down. My whole world had changed, and all because I'd said yes to a stranger.

Lesson: When things bottom out, it's time to take charge of your life and fly high.

Chapter 33

Madame Green asked me to put my hands on the crystal ball for a minute. She looked like my mother. Spooky. I took my hands off.

"Oh what a tangled web we weave, when we wish to lie and deceive," she said, looking at me intently with her piercing, brown eyes. Trina had warned me that she was good. I wanted to hide under the table. How did she know about John?

"Your husband has really gotten himself into a pickle, hasn't he?" I nodded. "He's gotten very good at lying and deceiving himself and others, but mostly himself. It's what he has to do to stay in the relationship that's not really of his choosing." I disagreed with her, but she continued anyway. "He knows they don't love each other, even if they say it. He seems to be letting her control a lot of things in their life. What do his letters say to you?" I wondered how she knew about the letters, but decided not to ask.

"Mixed. He loves me, and he doesn't know why he's acting like he does, and then he writes that we should move on from each other. Hasn't he? I know I have."

"His soul won't let him forget you. That's the problem. And she knows this. She gives him a hard time about you. She wonders why he married you. But he'll never marry her, and she seems to know this. She's a schemer and has a cruel mindset. She was born this way. Hopefully she can change it, but it's probably too late. Your family isn't happy with him either, and neither are his parents. They're ashamed that he's turned out this way. He's a very sweet person, or was. Inside he still is, but it's like he's detaching from who he really is. He's lost who he really is."

"Anything on Mark?" I asked, hoping to change the subject.

"Yes. A nice guy. Lots of fun. He's generous. He came at a good time in your life. He offers a different perspective. And he really likes you. You're the first genuine woman he's met in a long time. That's important to both of you. I see you dating other men here and there, but nothing serious. You and Mark will have a closer relationship. And who's Steve?"

"I don't know anyone by that name."

"Well, he's important. He's coming into your life soon. He'll help you a lot." I nodded.

"You mustn't divorce John, no matter what," she said seriously out of nowhere.

"Why?"

"I can't say for sure. But I wouldn't if I were you."

"I'm kind of tired of this limbo state I'm in. Are you sure about this?"

"I've never been more certain of anything in my life," she said quietly. I shuddered.

"There's a curtain surrounding what happened. You won't know for some time the truth of the matter. It would be easy for me to say he's in love and wants to marry her, but he doesn't. There's a lot more to this than meets the eye. Something strange is going on."

She stared out into space for several seconds.

"He sealed his fate the day he left you. A fateful mistake, but it's the path he chose. And decisions always have consequences. He will come back to you, but not in the way you think."

I thanked her for the reading, and as I was about to leave, she said again, "Remember. No divorce." I nodded.

Trina and I talked about my reading together at dinner that night.

"I could actually file papers for you. Or your dad could as well. I wonder why she said that, then."

"Because he might die after all? I hope so. It's been a couple months and I want this to be over with," I said between bites of my quiche.

"Most women hate their cheating husbands and want them dead. It's not unusual. The men are always surprised. Fools! They think what they did is excusable, but it's not. And some try to blame their wives who have done nothing wrong. If John heard you talk like this, I'm sure he'd agree too." She bit into her quiche. "This spinach quiche is good. We should have this again." I agreed.

"Did you open the letter he sent you? It's on the side

table." I got up and opened it.

"Well, he wants to see me when he comes to London. I wonder why?" I sat back down.

"He doesn't say?"

"No. Just his usual rubbish about how he misses me, and so on. I'm fed up with hearing it already," I continued eating and handed the letter to Trina. She read it carefully.

"So if he wants a divorce, your psychic therapists, as you call them, don't want you to do it. There has to be a hidden reason. Maybe you should try a couple of others, but they all seem to be saying the same thing." She set the letter on the table. "Are you going to see him?"

"I don't know if I should. I've started a new life. I really don't want him back. As you know, I'm not going backwards anymore," I finished my quiche and watched Trina eat. I took a sip of water.

"It'll be interesting to see how he reacts to you. I would see him just to get closure. Don't forget that we're going to that new nightclub tonight." I told her I was looking forward to it.

"The only way we're getting closure, is if we divorce or he dies. There is no other alternative. And until something happens, I'll always be in their relationship whether they want me there or not." I really was beginning to feel like Natalie. No wonder John wanted to live far away from me. I could easily show up and haunt both of them. He's lucky I didn't call all the time, or show up out of the blue. My integrity and pride would not let me stoop so low.

In two weeks, John showed up at Trina's place. I became anxious near the time he would show up. Trina went out on a date with a guy she met at the nightclub, and wouldn't be back for hours. I didn't know what to expect. But when I opened the door, he looked like the same John. We smiled politely and hugged awkwardly.

While hugging me, he said, "I *had* to see you. Please, please don't hate me. I couldn't live with myself if you did." I stepped away from him and stared at him.

"Are you kidding, John? Of course I hate you. You deliberately hurt me. There's no reason for you leaving me. And you won't tell me why you're doing this." I invited him in, but was not sure what to expect. He hadn't said anything about his reasons for coming.

We went into the living room to sit down and I poured some tea.

"I guess you'll always be mad at me then. It's a pity." He shook his head, sipping the tea.

"What is a pity is what you did. I have to ask this. Do you love her?" I looked at him closely, for John could never lie to me. He looked into my eyes.

"I'm fond of her," he said slowly.

"Are you happy?"

"I'm content, I guess." He nervously played with his coat sleeve. I knew he didn't like these questions, but I had a right to know the truth. I didn't think he was lying to me.

He had a hurt look in his eyes every time he looked at me. Yes, I was in their relationship and it was eating him up. One of the consequences of hurting others.

"That doesn't say much about your relationship. And I'll never understand what you're doing. You're throwing away a good relationship for a crappy one. I don't get it. She will never get you like I do, and I doubt she'll ever love you as much. But hey, that's your choice."

John leaned over and put his head in his hands. He looked miserable. I didn't care.

"Are you seeing anyone?" He looked up to ask me.

"Yes. As a matter of fact I am. Someone wealthy. He drives a Rolls Royce and owns boats and a plane. He does have the good life, and he's a nice guy." John looked even more distressed.

"So what becomes of us?"

"I don't know. I thought you would have filed divorce papers by now."

"I can't do that."

"Why?"

"I just can't. You're going to have to do it."

"John, I'm not doing that. You need to do it. You're the one who left and you need to get things in order." I totally forgot what Madame Green said, but I didn't care.

"You know you forced me to marry you, don't you?" He couldn't look at me when he said that.

I was taken aback. I couldn't believe what I just heard.

"No, John I didn't. You flew to me. Remember? You proposed to me. Remember? How quickly you forget, or are these the lies she feeds you to keep you in the relationship?" He didn't answer. "I thought so. You don't want to see it. Your eyes are closed and you're in a coma. You don't even know who you are anymore." I couldn't believe this was the same man I had married.

By now John didn't want to hear any more negative feedback. We were at a stalemate about what to do. But I knew one thing: John would never be able to return to me. At least not the man sitting across from me, who was a mere shadow of the man I used to know. And I wondered why a woman would live with a man who had so little potential. John had not changed; he continued to be the least likely man to succeed out there. I knew he was living in a slum area of Paris, but I didn't chide him for it. I bit my tongue.

"Can I ask what she sees in you?"

"What do you mean?" He seemed shocked.

"Well, you're not the best looking, most hardworking, or successful guy out there. So what's in it for her? Love? Please. Women don't hang on to someone who's not going to marry them or give them a better life. So why is she attached to you, do you think? You're secondhand goods. She's single, so why isn't she going after a rich guy?"

I could see that John was getting angry about this line of questioning, but I didn't care. He owed me an explanation. But then I realized that he didn't have one. He had no idea why he was with Marta, or what she really wanted. It was like a game. Only a game isn't funny when it affects other people's lives.

John got up to leave. He looked sad, but I ignored him when he apologized to me. Sorry does not cut it. He would have to make some serious amends. We hugged, then I watched him leave one more time. It was a bittersweet goodbye. I told myself it would be the last time I let him back in. He wanted to keep in touch, but I didn't understand why he would want to do that.

Wasn't he in a relationship? So strange!

I realized John had become a broken man, who needed to put himself back together again. That way he could save himself, just like the palm reader predicted.

Lesson: A person who lies and cheats has to live with their conscience. If they have one.

Chapter 34

After our most recent meeting, John was dead to me. And I wished he would die many times over. I begged the gods to make my dream come true. I sincerely hoped his parachute wouldn't open after all. If he died, I could give myself credit for being the one who got him started in the sport—a new way to kill your husband without lifting a finger. Drinks for everyone!

Trina and I were planning on doing some shopping. She believed that John had completely lost it. She thought he was playing both me and Marta, but I disagreed. I thought Marta was playing him, and he was trying to play me. But I wouldn't let him. He couldn't have both of us— she could have him. He wasn't worth keeping anymore.

As we walked along the streets of Piccadilly Circus, the bustling of cars and hordes of people everywhere in a hurry, reminded me of why I loved London so much. I felt I was in the center of the universe and everything was perfect. The energy was intoxicating, and it was pumping life into my battery so it would always be charged.

I stopped in front of a store front advertising massages. Chi Nei Tsang. I had no idea what that could be. Trina didn't know either, and wanted to keep moving. She left me there and said she would see me later. I nodded, staring at the sign. Suddenly, a man of short stature came out the door. His blue eyes sparkled and his face beamed at me. "Come in, come in. I've been expecting you." He took my arm gently and guided me to his office. I didn't know why, but I allowed him to do this. I trusted him completely.

"My name is Steve." He handed me paperwork to fill out. The psychic had been right!

"I'm Shawna." My eyes were transfixed on him as I started to fill out the paperwork. Only when I was done did I notice my surroundings. There was a medium-sized, brown desk with a phone and a stack of papers. Pictures of various Saints and gurus, most of them from East India, covered the walls. I noticed the large gold Buddha statue on the table. Flowers and a fountain were placed near it, and Chinese music of some kind played in the background. It was peaceful and serene.

Steve smiled and led me to his massage room. The room was light green with the same color carpet. One of the pictures on the wall appeared to be a painting of an other-worldly being with large blue eyes, a small nose and lips, and an enlarged head. The body was androgynous. I didn't know who it was, but it was beautiful and I couldn't take my eyes off it. Steve wouldn't tell me anything about it. He left while I removed all of my clothes except knickers, and climbed on top of the table. I had just pulled a blanket over me when he knocked and, at my invitation, came back into the room.

"I'm not doing Chi Nei Tsang on you yet. We need to get all the other junk out of your system first." He started massaging my back and seemed to find all kinds of emotional issues. "You have a lot of grief in your lungs. I'll help clear that. We carry issues lifetime after lifetime, and they get stuck. Time to get rid of them and put in more Christ light, or Buddha light, if you like."

Soon Steve was finding out all kinds of things that I considered private. He even knew some of my past lives. "You have blockage in your neck because you were beheaded twice. Once as Queen Anne in London with Henry VIII, and the other as a witch." That explains the London Tower. I was in awe of his healing hands, which seem to be shifting energy all over my body. I felt lighter and looser when we were done. And more relaxed.

"That was incredible. I've never had a massage. I feel great. More right with the world."

"Good. I need to see you once or twice a week for several weeks. Then Tibetan massage. Get several books as well. Here's a list. And continue meditating. It really helps you." I made my next appointment and started looking forward to the Tibetan massage.

I floated out of the building into the busy London streets, totally oblivious to all the noise and sights around me. I felt that I didn't have a care in the world. I was definitely on a new path.

By the time I got home, I had a bag of books. I noticed a letter from John that said he was moving, but he forgot to give me the address. He left a phone number, so I called him. A woman answered the phone, and I asked for John, but she didn't seem happy. I heard an angry voice talking to John in the background.

"Hi Shawna, what is it?" John asked, sounding slightly upset.

"I see you're moving and you didn't leave an address."

"Okay. Here it is." He gave me the address, then said, "Please don't call here. It upsets the woman we're living with." I wondered about this, but let the lie slide.

"I know she gives you a hard time about me, but that's the way it is." One of the consequences of bad behavior.

We said goodbye and hung up. I realized I had become the other woman in my own marriage, and laughed.

Lesson: Standing in Truth and Integrity nourishes your soul.

Chapter 35

After several weeks of massage, Steve wanted to do a spiritual treatment on me. I had no idea what to expect, but I was ready to try. Steve placed a mat on the floor, then had me lie down, supine. He covered me with blankets. The room was dimly lit and he added a couple of candles. He sat near me, cross-legged on a pillow. I was a little anxious, but I trusted that he had my best interests at heart.

I closed my eyes and did some breathing exercises. Soon, visual images started to show up.

"Where are you?" asked Steve.

"I'm on a hillside looking down at a village."

"Describe yourself."

I look down at my body and said, "I'm a boy about eleven years old, and my skin is light brown."

"What's on your feet?"

"I'm barefoot."

"What are you wearing?"

"A light-colored robe."

"Why are you on the hillside?"

"Because I did something bad. Something I never should have done." As I said this, my heart felt a lot of pain. Emotional pain."

"What did you do?"

"I'm a traitor. I betrayed my people." Now I felt the pain take over and it was deep. I remembered what I did and I was full of remorse. I thought of all the people I'd hurt, and I started sobbing. The pain was overwhelming now, and I couldn't stop crying. I wanted someone to kill me to take me out of the pain I felt. Intense sorrow and sadness consumed me. Steve was asking a question, but I couldn't answer. He asked another, but I ignored it and wondered why he couldn't see how upset I was. Suddenly he became very quiet. My soul seemed to suffer the most from this treatment. I cried uncontrollably for some time. Finally, I felt the emotions ease up a little bit. I stopped sobbing and took some deep breaths. I appeared to be in a totally dark place like a cave. I was safe here, so I could relax.

Finally Steve asked, "Do you see a light?"

I hesitated, but then noticed a light to my left. "Yes."

"Go to the light." As I got closer to the small light, it grew bigger and bigger. Soon it filled the entire cave and more. I covered my eyes to shield them from the brightness. The rays seemed to blast out everything I was feeling. As I entered the light, I only felt love and warmth. Loving arms held me. I tried to see a face or a figure, but all I could make out was an androgynous being. It looked translucent and its eyes matched the light it was sending out.

"What do you see?" asked Steve. I described the being

to him. It was like no other that I had ever experienced.

"How do you feel?" he asked.

"I only feel love. I never want to leave. I'm in total bliss." This was certainly a far cry from where I had just been. Steve let me bask in the light for some time. Eventually, he wanted me to leave, but I didn't want to.

"I could stay here forever."

"Yes, it's beautiful. But you need to return." I left, slowly devouring every drop of light, hoping it would fill my body and soul.

I lay with my eyes closed, knowing I needed to wake up. But I didn't want to. I opened my eyes and looked at Steve, who was watching me carefully.

"How was that?" he asked.

"Well, the first part I didn't like at all, but the second part was incredible. Who was that?"

"Who was that indeed? Who do you think it was?"

"I want to say mother/father God. A Supreme Being of some sort."

"Yes. And you can visit at any time. The light is always there for you. As for the first part, you need to forgive yourself."

"That will be hard." Just thinking about the incident brought back those feelings again. I hoped I wouldn't start crying, because I knew I wouldn't be able to stop. I thought of the light instead.

I stood up slowly. If I'd known what to expect, I don't

think I would have gone through with it. I told Steve that, and he smiled. Right. That's why he didn't tell me, and silly me for not asking.

Steve recommended that I drink a lot of water and be gentle with myself. Perhaps rest when I get home.

"You've had an astounding experience. Remember it. It will serve you well down the road. And I'll see you soon."

I hugged my guru. In spite of the beginning, the ending had been great.

I came out of the building expecting clouds like when I had gone in, but instead the sun had come out and shined down on me. I looked up and laughed. The gods must have been laughing, too.

Lesson: When you land in God, you are never the same.

Chapter 36

My life continued to get better and better. John and I communicated less frequently, and I actually began to hope he was happy. He didn't deserve it, but I tried to stay in my blissful state of light most of the time. That made me happy. I'd found a teacher who understood me and I didn't have to say a word. Priceless.

And Chi Nei Tsang, although painful, was causing major shifts in my body. Some subtle and some more intense. I'd had a shivering, cold experience that lasted for ten hours. After that it released blockages in my body. Most of them were emotional, and some were physical. But I was not prepared for the aftershocks of my current treatment.

I lay down on my bed and closed my eyes. Suddenly there was a spaceship in front of me. I got in and looked around. No one. I looked at the control panels and knew how to operate it. Soon I travelled at light speed far into the galaxies. I knew where to find home.

The beautiful, multicolored star system greeted me. Vibrant colors everywhere surrounded my home, like a huge rainbow engulfed the place. It was a star of creative energy, and we created well. Anything we wanted of the highest good. I disembarked the ship and there to greet me was every being occupying it. Thousands of them. I became so touched by their love and warmth that I wanted to cry. And everyone seemed to look alike. Androgynous, luminous beings came forward to welcome me home. It certainly wasn't a greeting you would receive on Earth. My parents came towards me and joined energies with me. I could tell them apart by their personalities. Telepathically they told me how much they loved and missed me. They were glad I was home, as was everyone else. At last, I was really Home. I couldn't read everyone's thoughts, but I felt that most that beings could read mine. Negative thoughts were not allowed on this place of Love, Peace, and Harmony. Celestial sounds of chimes and sing song voices seemed to fill the air. I felt my body vibrate to the rhythm of the sounds. Such a high, pure frequency that I knew so well.

After greeting everyone, my parents brought me to their home, which looked like a clear spaceship. I knew we didn't need shelter, food, sleep, or any other earthly necessity, so the ship must be to help me transition into my light body. My body started becoming lighter and more transparent.

"Welcome home dear one," said my mother. *"We missed you and we're glad you found your way back."* I was experiencing pure light, pure air, pure thoughts, and pure water—pure everything. Such a high frequency.

"I'm not going back to Earth. As you know, it is not

the best place for beings like us. It is too harsh of an atmosphere," I think to myself. My thoughts were becoming singsong as well.

"*We would not force you to do anything you don't want to do. We know it is a hard place. You must talk to the Council first. Although they cannot force you either,*" thought my father.

"*Do you know the experiences I've had on Earth?*"

"*Yes. We know. We know you have been going through some hard times.*"

"*Do you know John?*" They looked at each other, but their thoughts were private.

"*Yes. We do,*" my father communicated to me.

"*What about this other person?*"

"*We do not know that species. It is foreign and has a low frequency. We try hard to bring more light to Earth. It is a long ways away from us.*"

"*Am I being punished on Earth? It certainly feels like it sometimes.*"

"*No. Not ever. You choose the life, parents, body, sex, and all of that. It's interesting that you and John always said you could find each other no matter where you were on Earth. So congratulations. You found each other.*"

"*Is he going to die soon?*" My parents look at each other again.

"*We don't know. It's up to him really. There are some things he needs to do, so it could go either way.*" Now they were both thinking the same thoughts at the same time and singing them to me.

"*Did John come from here? I don't believe he did. There is too much light here and he chose darkness.*"

"*Yes, and all of it is a mystery. Even to us,*" they sang in unison.

"*Why don't you fly around your home and get acquainted again?*" My mother sang.

"*All right. I love you both.*" I hugged them by merging my light closer and closer to theirs. It felt wonderful.

I went outside to fly around. I found that I could blend in and out of the colors around me by thought. I felt light and joyful again—more so than I had ever been in my Earthly existence. I flew up to the highest mountain. It was purple with violet snow or some type of covering on top. If there was cold in this new place, it didn't bother me. I felt the same light temperature everywhere. I held out my hand and created a gold ball. I threw it up into the air and it soared like a rocket out of my reach. I laughed and chased it. I remembered this game. As I looked down, I saw the many colors surrounding my home. I wondered why I ever left. No one would want to leave here.

I was about to descend when a beautiful unicorn showed up. I asked if I could ride her, and she nodded. I mounted easily and still carried the ball that I caught in my hand. And off we went. I realized she was taking me back to the Council—it was time to meet them. It seemed like I had just gotten here. But there was no time here, so I had no idea how long I'd been Home.

She dropped me off in front of a massive white building with large round pillars and many steps. It reminded me of Greek architecture and as I thought that, I saw Socrates, or someone who looked like him, standing near me. He was in a light body now, but I recognized him. He greeted me and wanted to escort me in. Judgment Day, I thought.

"Not Judgment Day. Your day. You get to make your case for staying here. It's a big day."

"And I have not prepared. I should get a lawyer."

"You are a lawyer, among all the other occupations you've had. All you need is to tell the truth."

"That's easy. If that's all I need to do, how did I end up back on Earth?"

"Let's just say you tricked yourself into going back. But you also tricked the Elders."

"How so?"

He just smiled, and soon I was standing in front of twelve beings who looked like me, and sent love to me. Yes. I remembered them well. They sat in a half circle.

"We are so glad you are here. Would you like to sit, stand, or hover?" Telepathically I heard them.

"I'll hover." I glided into the air and looked down on them. I liked being above them, even if it was just barely. I

could only fly so high.

"I'm not going back to Earth, and you can't make me." I thought loudly to them. They smiled and glanced at each other. I did not know their thoughts.

"That is fine. We don't think you should go either. Earth is too heavy for you."

"So if I don't go back then what? Are there consequences? And if so, what kind?"

"There are always some consequences. In this case, you didn't complete your mission that you set out to do. This is your last life on Earth, as you know. You keep telling everyone that. It's a good reminder for you and us. We think you should return to keep your promise, but that is entirely up to you."

"Keeping promises is all I've ever done. I don't see that working so well."

"Promises are meant to be kept and there are huge penalties for not doing so. Spiritual penalties. They can be severe, depending on the promise."

"So what is my penalty if I don't return?"

"You may have to return to Earth one final time. I know you don't want that. No one does. You could be forced to go to a lower level planet or star for a certain length of time. There is also solitary confinement, and various other things that we won't go into. However, we would like to show you a movie of your life should you decide to return. That way you can make an informed

decision."

I watched as a film about my life appeared on the wall behind them. I watched everything, looking for clues of a less than ideal life. I saw myself working in a hospital and various clinics, helping a lot of people. I saw a good-looking man by my side, and we lived in a huge house near water. I saw myself traveling all over, skiing, dancing, riding in hot air balloons, and hiking mountains. Suddenly, the movie disappeared.

"If you go back your life does get better. It hasn't been a disaster, but you remembered a lot as a child, and now you know even more. You help a lot of people. I know that's one of the reasons you went back. You wanted to experience negativity again, since everything here is positive, and for you that can be a little boring at times."

"It's boring on Earth, too, you know. Here, I can create more."

"Take your time."

I thought about the life I would be living, and made a decision.

"Who is this man I'm going to meet?"

"He is someone you haven't seen for a long time. Egypt. You two create great things together. And he waits for you."

"Fine. I'll go. Against my better judgment. Again." I realized I wanted completion in my Earthly life, and to meet this new man. He intrigued me.

"Just remember, your light is Fierce. One of the reasons you went back was to help others and show them their own light within. You do it well. So it is good. We support your decision and can't wait for you to return." As I turned to leave, I heard in the distance, *"Just because he's young, don't turn away from him."* I wanted to turn back to ask about that, but it was too late. I opened my eyes and I was back in London. I clenched the bed covers in my hands, and cursed myself for doing this again. When will I ever learn?

Lesson: An inner demon can turn out to be your greatest ally. It can force you to seek out your True Home. One you will never want to leave.

Chapter 37

I got up and went to the kitchen to make some tea. I couldn't believe how wonderful my home was, or that I had come back here. The thought made me want to cry, and I knew if I started it would last for a long time. Instead, I thought of my date tonight with Mark.

Trina came in from work, all dressed in her raingear and umbrella. She shook it out and opened it up to dry. She took off her shoes and said, "So how's it going? Did you have your session today?"

"Yes." I forced a smile. She came over to look at me.

"Your face looks luminous. What have you done? It's very bright looking."

"Must be my new makeup." I didn't like lying, but I didn't want to explain. At least, not yet.

"I must try it. Can I have a cup of tea?"

"Yes." I poured tea for us.

"Did you go skiing yesterday? I've never understood dry hill skiing. Doesn't it hurt when you fall?" She took a sip of tea and we sat at the kitchen table.

"Yes. It does hurt, which is why I'm only skiing on snow from now on."

"I know you keep in touch with your family. Have they said how they feel about John?"

"Don't get my dad started. My mom doesn't like to say unkind things about other people, but they're disappointed. As am I." I thought of my real family and just wanted to go Home again. The very thought made me want to cry. I missed everyone already.

Trina picked up a spoon and pretended it was a microphone. She wanted to change the subject and coerce me out of my sad state.

"Tell us, Shawna. How does it feel to be dating London's most eligible bachelor, Mark Spencer?" She smiled at me and told me to look into a pretend camera. She pointed the spoon to my mouth so I could talk into it.

"Well, he's wonderful Trina. A great companion and full of surprises."

"And what's the sex like?"

"Well Trina, I don't like to kiss and tell, but like the cars he drives, he knows when to slow down and when to accelerate. And he always leaves me satisfied." At this we both laughed and she put the spoon down.

"You're so lucky. Isn't he flying you to Paris tonight?"

"I don't think so, if it's raining."

"It's going to stop by the time you leave. I'm sure it's fine. Plus, doesn't he like to take chances?"

"Just not in the plane. Boats, he will be more adventurous. But we'll see." I sip my tea.

"Have you decided about your future?"

"Yes. I'm buying my ticket home tomorrow. I can't

believe I'm finally leaving London. I don't know why I'm leaving, but I feel I need a change."

"I'm going to miss you. It's been fun with all the parties and nightclubs. When are you leaving?"

"In about four weeks. I will miss you, too! And all the shopping and nightclubs we've gone to. And I have a date on my calendar for when I'm getting divorced, no matter what the psychics have said. I'm done. I need my freedom."

"Good for you. Your dad is going to represent you, I suppose."

"Yes. And he's looking forward to it. It will bring him great pleasure."

"Wow! Things are moving around." Just then the phone rang. It was Mark confirming our plans and said the weather was fine now. I called Lyn to let her know dinner was a go in Paris.

"You're going to miss Mark and all these great dates," Trina said with a grin.

"I know. I will miss him. He's so good to me. I can't believe we've been going out for ten months already."

"You should get ready for your date."

I tried to move, but couldn't. I was thinking of how much I would miss these talks with Trina.

"I shouldn't plan events after my massages because I never know what might hit me. I already had one episode and I don't want another one tonight. I'll explain later on."

"Are you going to your therapist tomorrow? I might

go with you."

"She's new to me. Reads Turkish coffee. I'll call her and let her know that you're coming with me."

"Great. I've never had that done before."

"What are you doing tonight?" I asked as I got up to get ready.

"I have a case I'm working on. I might go out to the pub after that."

"I'd invite you with us if we weren't meeting Lyn and Pierre. They made the reservations."

"It's okay, really. I can't anyway. But thanks." For the first time, I heard envy in Trina's voice. I always envied her life as a successful lawyer living in London. Ironic.

By the time Mark showed up, I had dressed in a sexy black dress that he liked. I put on the diamond necklace he had given me and brushed my hair. I'd come a long way.

We flew to Paris and met Lyn and Pierre at a fancy French restaurant they favored. Lyn seemed particularly excited to see me. She had wanted to tell me something on the phone but left it for tonight. So after we ate and drank, she made an excuse to use the restroom and I went with her.

"Okay. You're dying to tell me something. What is it?" We sat in the big, cushy chairs in the lounge area, away from the restroom.

"Am I going to like this?" I leaned in to look at her.

"Not sure. I saw John yesterday and talked to him." I

let that sink in.

"Okay. And?" She paused until a woman walking by us made her way out of sight.

"Well, we hug and I ask him how things are. He puts on this forced smile and says 'fine', but I know he's miserable. He says he made a big mistake leaving you. He says he'll regret it until his dying day."

"I refuse to feel sorry for him. He made a terrible choice."

"Did he ever? Anyway, he says I'll probably find out sooner or later, so he tells me she's pregnant." When Trina says this, I'm glad I'm sitting down. I'm surprised by the news. John had always been careful about that, so this seems hard to believe. Especially given their financial situation.

"So I say to him, 'How do you know it's yours?' I'm cheeky at times. He says he's not one hundred percent sure, but since he's with her he's kind of stuck."

Now I'm laughing. "He got himself into this mess. And he doesn't like to be trapped. It's going to be interesting to see how he gets out of this one." Lyn just smiled at me.

"I know. He's such an idiot. And she's desperate and using every trick in the book to keep him, which means?"

"Which means she doesn't think she can keep him, unless there's something else holding them together. Like a baby. Which doesn't work either. That is such a con. I wish women would quit doing that. It gives us all a bad name, not to mention sleeping with married men. That does as well."

"I know. Well he got involved with a liar, a whore, and who knows what else. She's a disgrace to the female gender."

"I don't feel sorry for him. I really don't. I hope he's miserable with her until the end of time. It's what he deserves. And that's just for starters."

"Yeah. Why are men so stupid? Except for Pierre, of course." She shrugged.

"Right. Mark is not like this either. When we're together, we're together. We only sleep with each other. Hey! I should have a baby. Now he has to marry me. And hate me for the rest of my life. No thanks." I shook my head at that very thought. The idea of emotional blackmail never appealed to me.

"So John hasn't asked you for a divorce?"

"No. That is weird. You'd think he'd do the honorable thing, but I guess he really doesn't want to marry her. Interesting. It's funny. He said I forced him to marry me, and now who's doing the forcing? He should really have listened to the lies she fed him. Now he's going to suffer for it."

"How so?" Lyn leaned in to look at me.

"So when he said I forced him, he was repeating what she'd told him. John knew better. He couldn't even look at me when he said it. Now *she's* trying to force him to marry her."

"It's a mess. I don't know how he plans to get out of it. Decisions, decisions. You're right though. He's not going to divorce you. He'd have done it by now. My husband owes us money from that bet we made some time back."

"Maybe now the psychics will change their minds about this divorce. I have a date on my calendar for it, so we'll see." I knew inside the psychics probably saw his death, and didn't want to tell me. Why else would they give me the advice that they did? Still I grew tired of waiting.

"Let me know how that goes. I'll keep you informed on this side."

Lesson: Listening to your Ego will steer you in the wrong direction, but your Higher Self will steer you on the right path.

Chapter 38

In my dream I am hitchhiking on a road. The surrounding area reminds me of the countryside of France. A small, blue Volkswagen stops beside me to give me a ride. I open the door and then realize it's John, and he is smiling at me. I slam the door and start walking away. He follows me while driving the car, begging me to talk to him. I refuse, and then tell him to leave me alone. Finally, he gets out of the car and stands in front of me. He puts his hands on my shoulders to keep me still. I look at him and say, *"What do you want?"*

He sighs and says, *"I'm going to make things right. You'll see. I have a plan, for both of us."*

"I don't believe you. When have you ever done the right thing?"

"Marrying you was the right thing."

"That's not what you said the last time."

"I was wrong. I've been listening to a voice I shouldn't have. I should be listening to myself. And now I've ruined everything."

"Yes, you have."

"Please don't hate me. I want to be the man you traveled with and married, not this guy I don't even recognize."

"You have a lot of make up for. I hope you know that."

"I do. And I do it gladly if you and I stay connected. I can't let you go. It drives her crazy. And now things have gotten worse."

"I see that. I hear a baby is on the way. You should be so proud." I say this sarcastically and roll my eyes.

"It's not what I wanted. I will find a way out. I give my word. And I know you don't trust what I say anymore, and I have to prove myself to you."

"We'll see then."

We hug each other and I look into John's sad eyes. He puts up a good front, but inside he's dying.

I told Trina about the dream on the tube as we made our way to this new seer. She hoped John would keep his promise this time.

Lady Bennu was waiting for us in her living room. She had a short stature with shoulder length dark hair and black eyes that bore through me. She was wearing a long, flowing blue dress, and she instructed each of us to drink the Turkish coffee that was sitting on the table. She asked if we wanted a reading together or apart. Since Trina and I have no secrets, we agreed to joint readings. She read Trina's first, and Trina was astounded at how accurate it was. She was happy about her new future, too. I was delighted for her. Then Lady Bennu read for me. She talked about John and his predicament. She saw a good future for me. She saw me married within a year. I was surprised to hear this.

"Am I getting divorced then?"

"No. I don't see that," she shook her head.

"Then he dies, is that correct?" I thought of my dream.

"No. I don't see that. I see an accident. It's pretty bad." I knew she was lying, because how else would I be getting married? I remember the divorce date on my calendar.

"When will this happen?"

"In the near future. Closer than you think." I already felt tension and relief from her words. Then she added, "Whatever you do, don't change your travel plans." I thought to myself that I would never do that anyway.

"And you'll have money in the near future, as well." I thought of my insurance policy.

We both paid and left. Astounded by her news, I said, "I wonder if this is his way out."

"Might be. I'm sure it's still an accident. Fate stepping in to correct a problem."

"I wonder why now? Why not months ago?"

"I don't know. Maybe he had to be desperate enough to get out of it. And now he is."

Three weeks later, I was making a packing list for my trip. The phone rang, and it was John's father.

"I don't know if you've heard the news or not."

I answered in the negative, surprised to hear from him. He was speaking very bluntly, as usual.

"John's been killed in a skydiving accident. The plane crashed and burned. He was the only one who didn't make it out."

Although I was expecting this, I sat down, speechless.

"Are you still there?" he asked.

"Yes. So what happens now?"

"Well, the medical examiner has cremated the body. Here's the number for you to call. We're all in shock, as you can imagine. No one was expecting this."

Except me, I thought to myself.

We said goodbye and hung up. I had not heard from John's family in a long time. They didn't want to be in the middle of John's situation or take sides. I understood.

I was still stunned by the news. Lady Bennu was wrong about his accident, although I knew she didn't want to give bad news. Or in this case, good news. My dream had taken way too long to materialize, but it did come true, just under different circumstances.

I called Lyn to see if the incident was on the news. She said she'd call me back.

"Yes. It's on the news. Apparently he bought a new parachute and this was his first jump in it. I'm sorry, although it's a bittersweet ending. You're a free woman now. That must make you feel good, but he's gone now. Never to be seen again. No, you see him in your dreams.

Maybe he'll visit you like he said he would."

I was silently processing the information. "Well he's coming back to me, just not the way I thought." Underneath, I always thought John would finally get out of the darkness and remember what we had. I knew it was a long shot, which is why I went on with my life, as if nothing had happened between us. But love between soul mates is hard to forget.

"If you want, I can pick up the ashes and send them to you." Lyn was always generous.

"You know what? Why don't you send them to his parents? I'll give you the address. It's the right thing to do. Even though I know what to do with some of those ashes, but better I don't have them."

Lyn chuckled and said, "Yeah, I don't want you clogging up Trina's loo. I'll get on this right now. And take care of yourself. I'm glad you have lots of friends in London to help you through this. And if you want, I can fly out and be with you."

"No. You don't have to. I'm fine, really. But it's sweet of you to offer."

We hung up. I told Trina what happened.

"Wow! So how do you feel?" She came over and put her arms around me.

"I can't seem to cry and I think that's a good thing. The John I knew died a long time ago."

"Well, I don't want you to be alone. So I'm taking you

out tomorrow night. And if you need anything, I'm here."
Trina was such a good friend.

I called everyone I knew to tell them the news. My family was concerned about me, but I could sense their relief as well. For me, I finally got the closure I needed.

I went into my room and picked up John's guitar. I lovingly played it and then I started to cry.

Lesson: Someone's death can be the best thing that ever happened to you.

Chapter 39

My final week in London was spent going out with friends to pubs and nightclubs. I felt sad and glad at the same time. My emotions seemed to be a roller coaster, but I kept myself under control. I didn't cry anymore, and most of the time, I just felt glad it was over. Mark took the news in stride. We would always be friends. I would miss London. And Paris had redeemed herself by taking John. She was forgiven for letting a dark force have him. In the end, it had been a good thing we never got divorced. She never deserved to have him. John's life started and ended with me, as he had predicted.

My friend Mary and I decided to take a walk after eating lunch. Mary and I had worked together, and had gone out to pubs and football games. We talked about America as we walked towards the Hammersmith Odeon Theatre. I saw a couple walk towards us, and for some reason I kept staring at the woman. I thought I recognized her. Her beautiful energy reached out and touched me as if caressing my soul. We seemed deeply connected for no apparent reason. She glanced at me and smiled. In that spit second she grabbed my heart and soul. I glanced over at her husband and gasped, Paul and Linda McCartney. I felt like I'd been touched by a Light Being, and as I walked away, I had a new hero.

London is full of surprises, which is why it's such a fun place to live. But more was in store for me as Trina gave me a going away party. That turned out to be a great time, but it also made me homesick for London, even though I hadn't even left yet. I couldn't believe I was leaving. I loved it here, but it was time for me to go home, and go to school, if nothing else.

While we cleaned up after the party, I said to Trina, "I think it's strange that John died shortly after I bought my airline ticket. And he died the month we met in Paris. I don't think the same day though, but I'll have to check. It's like it started a wheel in motion."

"I hadn't thought of that. But now that you mention it things are moving quickly," she says as we start washing and drying the dishes.

As if it all needs to be wrapped up nice and neat. John created a mess and... and... he finally cleaned up the mess." I realized John had finally done the right thing for a change. I was beginning to think he wasn't so bad after all. I was drying the dishes while Trina washed.

"The hurt of what he did will fade fast, if it hasn't already. But you had a great life here for ten months, or whatever it was."

"I met my guru, who's moving back to America. I plan to see him there."

"And I'm supposed to marry an American and move

there. How great is that!" Trina beams as she washes a plate.

"We'll be neighbors. Unless I move somewhere else. Who knows? Our future awaits us." With John dying, I actually felt I had a future for a change. I don't know how the two of them could live like they did? No concrete future, no history, and not much of a present. Weird. I finish drying the last item and answer the phone.

It's John's father informing me of the Memorial Service. I hang up and laugh.

"Shawna, what is *so* funny?" she asks, putting the soap away and coming into the living room.

"That was John's dad letting me know about John's service. And guess what?" Now I'm in hysterics. "It's the same day I'm flying to America." I finally get the sentence out.

"This keeps getting more bizarre. He's probably not the father of the baby either. Now *that* would be ironic."

"I wouldn't put it past her. Nothing she does surprises me anymore. After all, we know she's willing to screw around with married men, so she has no morals. Anything to get a ring on her finger. Anything to win. I'm glad I'm not like that." I look at Trina and grin. "Gee, what does that say about her?"

"So true. It's a shame, really. I feel sorry for children brought into the world like that. It's not right at all. There should be a law, I say. And maybe I'll run for office on that alone."

"I'd vote for you." And with that we said goodnight and walked to our bedrooms.

The next day Mark dropped in to say goodbye. He has a present for me, he said, but won't tell me what it is. We made our way outside, and there by the curb was the Rolls Royce with a bow on top of its black roof. I turned to Mark.

"You're not giving me this, are you?" My eyes were wide and my heart was racing.

He held out the keys to me and says, "Yes. However there is a catch. You have to come back to claim her. She's no good in America with steering on the wrong side and all that."

I became overjoyed and close to tears at the same time. Such generosity. I rushed over and wrapped my arms around the car. I did love it. The best gift *anyone* has ever given me. But I know I can't accept it. I'm probably not coming back, even though I have a return ticket. I walked back to him and kissed him, and then hugged him tightly. I lucked out in meeting this incredible person.

"Don't ever change. You are the best. And I love you. Thank you so much," I whispered in his ear as my eyes filled with tears.

"I love you too. Come back to London," he whispered back.

"I'll think about it," I replied. We went for a ride in the car, then said our goodbyes. I realized how much I would miss him, as well as London. The last week had been phenomenal.

Lesson: Rewards happen to those who wait patiently. And they come in many disguises.

Chapter 40

I was finally going home. London and her people had taught me so much. I felt grateful and humbled by the gifts—especially the spiritual ones. I picked up my backpack and John's guitar. I couldn't leave it behind, even though I thought I could. I reluctantly carried it on my right shoulder and walked to the subway.

In the subway, I saw a young man playing his old guitar with the case open for money. He was playing a song that John and I always liked, "Stairway to Heaven" by Led Zeppelin. I listened for a few seconds, then took off the guitar and opened it in front of him. He stopped playing and watched me.

"You can have it. I don't need it anymore." Before he could refuse, I said, "Today is your lucky day." As I walked quickly away, I heard him thank me, and I felt much lighter.

The flight was uneventful. I had mixed feelings about being back in Miami. John and I had lived here as well, so there were some memories I would have to cope with.

My dad picked me up at the airport and wanted to know about London. Eventually, we got on to the subject of John. "Is it too painful to talk about?" he asked while driving.

"No. Not really." I told him about the psychic's predictions and my dream.

"I didn't know your intuition was that strong? It's a good thing. It'll come in handy when you're a lawyer." He winked at me as he spoke.

"I do plan to go to school. No more talking. However, probably medical school."

"That's fine. You don't belong in the computer world. I don't know if Gina told you, but she's thinks she'll marry this guy she's been going out with. He seems nice and is an accountant. We'll see."

"I'm happy for her. She finally met a man she's not too nitpicky about."

"You taught her a good lesson."

"Which is?"

"Don't marry guys with little money and ambition. A good lesson for most women, wouldn't you say?"

"I agree. Or if you marry them, prepare to be the breadwinner. And it's not a fun role. Also, find someone with strong willpower and self-esteem."

"I never understood why he did this. Do you? I mean, what was that relationship about really?"

"I'm not one hundred percent sure, but I think he got caught up in his ego. Another woman wants him. He must be hot. And yet John never seemed to be like that. He always said cheating was against his nature. She was a horrible person, and he became one as well." It would be years before I learned the truth of the situation.

I unpacked my clothes in my room and realized I wanted to be on my own again. I would have enough money to move to California and that was my new plan.

Before I knew it, I was walking on the beach. The sun was shining, birds were singing, and the ocean's waves tempted me into the water. I took off my sandals and rolled up my pants. I walked into the water and strolled along the edge. I stopped suddenly. I hadn't planned to be here. I looked at the spot where John and I had said our wedding vows. I stared at it, and then saw John's image wearing his blue tuxedo. While I looked at him, a young woman walked by me, holding her radio. She smiled at me and I returned the favor. She started singing the song her radio was playing. It was the Beatles, "All You Need Is Love." When I looked up, John was gone.

Lesson: Life is a joke and as soon as you get that, you will laugh and laugh and never stop.

Epilogue:
John Speaks

After years of dreams, mediums, Akashic record readings, and visits by John, I finally received some answers.

In this dream I am falling. Suddenly, a person scoops me up and we arrive on a mountain top. It's John, and he takes my hand and sits on a rock with me on his lap. I don't want to be with him, but I'm curious to hear what he has to say.

"*I'm sorry for everything that's happened. I am full of remorse. I love you,*" he says with those soulful eyes of his. They don't melt me like they used to.

"*So I need to know what happened and why?*" I ask. He wants me to drop it but I won't. With our soul groups, guides, and higher selves present, he explains.

"*I take full responsibility for my role with her. But it wasn't totally my fault.*"

"*Whose fault was it then?*"

"*Hers. I got sideswiped. She manipulated me.*"

"*How did she do that?*"

"*Our contracts got changed. This wasn't supposed to have happened.*"

"*Our sacred contracts that we signed before coming*

here?" I ask. *"That's not possible."*

"There was a glitch in the program so to speak. So, it wasn't entirely my fault."

"You still didn't have to leave. If my contract changed, I would have ignored it. I'm a married person. I'm not supposed to do this. How hard is it to say no to someone?"

"I know. I should have stayed. But I died to put things right. I think I should get some credit for that." He looks at me again. *"The big fluke was the cog in the wheel that was vampiric in nature. I hope you can forgive me and understand."*

"I always said she was evil and you didn't believe me. You're so egotistical when you are human. So you could have done the right thing, and yet you didn't?"

"I stand in honesty and integrity about that. That I shouldn't have done it. I wasn't as strong as you. And strong women are always a threat to a male ego. As for her, I was a game to her. I let myself be a pawn. If I had to do it over again, of course I wouldn't. I wanted to leave, but always got pulled back in. Emotional blackmail."

"And now you get to make amends. How fun!" I look at John to see how sad and hurt he is about everything he's done.

"I will make amends to you, starting with this book. It's a gift from me to you. I felt your suffering and pain and lived it for a time. Plus my own. Imagine a wheel and

then a dark force who has jealousy and animosity in her heart. She put a stake in the wheel. And along with that the Dark Lord of Time does not like the new paradigm. Too much light and love coming to the planet, and he also allowed this to happen. The glitch has been fixed, and it will never happen again."

"Thank you for your honesty and integrity. I know she has none. Too bad." I say, touching John's hair. He holds me tighter.

"You and I are Soul Brother and Sister. We are Star Family, and have been together a long, long, time. I love you so much. You are my Lover and Beloved. And all of the children we had were not in vain."

"Are several of our children on our Star?" I am starting to feel more love for John than I had in some time.

"Yes. They send love and greetings."

"That's nice to hear. I wish I could remember them all. Just so you know, I'm not returning to earth again. Ever. And this time I mean it. I'm staying in the pure frequency of light where I belong. I came to help humans here, and I've been doing that. But I belong in the ethers, playing with the Masters. And besides I don't belong on Earth. My inner demon is my best ally now."*

"I know. I'm your best cheerleader. Remember, I'm going to keep visiting you and we can always meet in dream time. I have to go now, my beloved. I'll be waiting for you time after time."*

With that, John gently kisses me and disappears.

I take a better look at my surroundings, and it seems so familiar to me. The colors are vibrant and beautiful. I look at the violet sky. I know where I am. Love, Peace, and Harmony. John had brought me *Home*.

Thanks for reading. If you have any comments or questions, please feel free to email me at shawnacjones@pobox.com

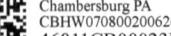
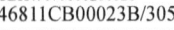